LOVE CAN BE A
DANGEROUS GAME 2

JAZ' AKINS

MZ. LADY P PRESENTS, LLC

Love Can Be a Dangerous Game 2

Copyright © 2017 by Jaz' Akins

Published by Mz. Lady P Presents

All rights reserved

www.mzladypresents.com

❀ Created with Vellum

1

KADENCE

Bryson stood there with a confused look on his face.

"Like y'all planned? What the hell?" He rubbed his hands over his dreads and stared at me. "You don't have amnesia?" I struggled to find the words. Jazelle had put on gloves and taken the gun from my hands.

"Not to be rude or anything, but are you helpin' or naw? We got to get out of here. Y'all can figure this shit out later." I knew Jazelle was pissed about Bryson and me. We had this shit planned down to a tee, and then shit went left. Me getting pregnant was not a part of the plan. My fuckin' daughter was almost nine. What the hell I look like starting over. Me getting shot was also not a part of the fuckin' plan. That shit was unexpected. I knew Loyal would be upset, but the thought of him shooting me never crossed my mind. Bryson looked back and forth between Jazelle and me.

"What the hell did y'all have planned?"

"I'll explain everything later, but right now, we got to get this body out of here. There's proof that Jazelle bonded him out. She's going to be the first suspect."

"Why not you?" Bryson cut me off.

"Because I'm the innocent wife who can't remember anything.

Loyal has been cheating on me for years. The whole world knows it. They also know I was just released from the hospital because he tried to kill me." Bryson looked at Jazelle.

"And y'all planned all of this?" Jazelle nodded her head.

"That's kind of what we do for a living. Set up niggas who don't deserve the shit they have." Bryson looked like his mind had been blown. He took off his shirt and threw it on the counter.

"Man, can you get his feet?" He said, staring at Jazzy. I smiled as Bryson and Jazelle lifted Loyal's limp body from the floor. I ran and opened the door that leads out to the garage. I popped the trunk Jazelle's car, and they folded him inside.

"Okay, so what do I do with this until Devon makes it here?" Jazelle said as she jumped in the car and opened the garage door

"Just drive there and wait. You got a better chance of getting in trouble if you're in the streets. Devon won't be long." I rushed her. I knew she wanted Bryson, but that shit was dead. I turned and looked at Bryson who was already staring at me.

"I thought I was about to get some pussy." He pouted. I smiled and wrapped my arms around him.

"I can do that. But first, let's get the fuck out of here." I grabbed his hand and walked out of the garage, closing the door behind us. Bryson climbed into the driver's seat. As soon as we were both in the car, Bryson started in with the questions.

"So this was all a set up to kill Loyal?" He stared at me.

"No, not all of it. The plan was to get rid of Loyal in a way that Kai and I would still be good. I have money saved, but it wasn't enough. All I know how to do is be a musician's wife and a stick-up kid. He tried to kill me first, Bryson. He tried made a fool of me too many times." I fought the urge to cry.

"Are you going to kill me too?" Bryson cleared his throat.

"No. Why would I do a thing like that?" I pulled down the visor to check my makeup.

"Do you love me?" I looked at him and smiled.

"Of course I do."

"Remember when I said I couldn't deal with my girl lying to me?" I nodded my head scared of where this conversation was going.

"I couldn't tell you. I had to wait until everything was done. There was so much shit going wrong that I couldn't risk it." Bryson sucked his teeth and glanced at me. He drove through the quiet streets, with his jaws clenched.

"From here on out, no more secrets. We're still a family, ain't we?" I stared at him. Bryson nodded his head but said nothing. His phone started to ring, and he ignored it.

"Who was that?" I was now turned around in my seat, facing him.

"Nobody important." Bryson turned the music up.

He drove to the Radisson and parked in front. "You do whatever you have to do with Jazelle in my car. I'm expecting some ass when you get back." Bryson smiled at me letting me know that everything was okay between us. I leaned in and kissed him with everything I had in me.

"I'll be right back." He got out of the car, and I pulled off. I dialed Jazelle's number. She answered the phone, her voice dripping with attitude.

"How long am I supposed to wait with a fucking body, Kay?"

"Until she gets there. What do you want me to do?"

"Can you hop off Bryson and call and see where she is?" I decided to let her smart remark go.

Without another word, I hung up the phone and dialed Devon's number. She didn't answer so I just kept driving to the spot where we were supposed to meet. I turned up the music. Tink's "Rachet Command-ments" blared through the speakers. The sun was shining, and for a second it seemed like everything was right in the world, except for the fact that I had just murdered my husband. Loyal had pushed me to the point that I didn't know who I was anymore. And, when I found myself, it told me that motherfucka had to go! He had already shown me that moving on was not an option, so Jazelle's drunk babbling started to make sense to me. I pulled into the parking lot of the abandoned warehouse on the outskirts of town. Jazelle jumped out of her car and into Bryson's truck.

"He let you drive this fuckin' truck?" I ignored her and dialed Devon's number. She answered in her usual way.

"Whassup baby?"

"Where are you? We're here waiting." I looked over at Jazelle who rolled her eyes.

"I'm inside. Pull the door open." Jazelle's face turned bright red.

"Are you fucking kidding me?" she screamed and got out of the car. She walked to the huge garage door and slid it open. She then jumped back in her car and pulled inside. I followed her into the garage and shit off my engine.

"You okay, Jazzy?" I put my hand on her shoulder, and she halfway smiled.

"Yeah, I'm fine. I'm glad you are too. You had me shook for a minute, sis." I smiled and hugged my best friend. I had missed her while all of the drama was happening. I doubted if things would ever be like they were, but this was better than what they had been recently. Devon walked out looking like a black Barbie. She swung her long blond hair over her shoulder.

"Whassup baby?" She smiled and winked at Jazelle. "What y'all got for me?" I pointed to Jazelle's Beamer, her pride and joy.

"Get rid of it and everything inside it." Devon rubbed her hands together and walked over to the car.

"Something or somebody?" I smiled, and Devon nodded her head and took the keys from Jazelle.

"You gone take me out while I'm in town?" She grinned at Jazelle who turned and walked towards Bryson's truck.

"I keep telling you I'm strictly dickly." Devon walked up behind her opening the passenger door for her.

"That's what they all say 'til the get that first taste."

Jazelle buried her head in her hands clearly embarrassed. I couldn't help but laugh. As much of a freak as she claimed to be, you would think a woman would not have her so bent out of shape. Devon loved it. She saw Jazelle as a challenge and if I didn't know any better. I'd say she was making progress.

"I'll send you my bill."

"Okay, thanks love." I got in the truck and put on my seatbelt. Jazelle kept looking at me and smacking her lips but said nothing.

"Whassup?" I asked, hoping she would finally speak her mind and cut it with the extra ass hints she was dropping.

"So this thing with Bryson, it's like a real thing?"

"I don't know. Was it a real thing when you were fucking my husband?" Jazelle took another deep breath and stared out the window. I knew that was a conversation she wasn't willing to have because that would mean admitting she had fucked up.

"Can you just drop me off at home please?" She stuck her earbuds in her ear and continued to stare out the window. I turned the music back up completely unbothered by the attention she was so desperately begging for. When I pulled in front of her house, Jazelle jumped out and ran inside without a word.

"I ain't got time for this bitch."

I backed out of the driveway and raced back to the hotel to make love to Bryson. I knew all too well what leaving your man horny could bring your way, and I didn't want any repeats.

2

JAZELLE

I was glad this shit was finally over. As far as I was concerned, Kadence and I never had to pull off another hit again. This one had taken everything in me. Now here I was riding around with a dead body, Loyal's dead body in my trunk. Devon had agreed to meet us at a spot she had here in town, but it seemed like the 15-minute drive was taking forever. Anything was better than watching Bryson and Kadence be all in love. The shit was sickening! I never meant for Bryson to be affected by any of this.

"I don't know how long I'll survive this marriage, sis. This shit is killing me!" Kadence stared at me on the verge of tears. I took a sip of Hennessy and stared at her.

"Well, I been told you to leave his ass. You're suffering because you want to. Loyal is anything but fuckin' loyal. Matter of fact, why is that even his damn name?" Kadence smiled for the first time since she had walked in.

"Where I'mma go, Jazzy? Anybody's house I go to he can find me. I don't work and I never been to college, so I have no skills. All I know is how to take care of people. How can I live without my husband?" She buried her head in her hands and cried.

I picked up my phone to call Ashlee, my weed person. That was the only way we would make it through this night. I poured up both shots of Remy and sat down next to Kadence. She downed both shots and handed the empty glasses back to me.

"Can I have some more?" Kadence hiccuped and giggled while I grabbed the bottle and sat it on the floor between the two of us. I refilled the shot glasses and stared at Kadence.

"Why don't you just kill him?" I said in between giggles. Kadence looked up at me with a huge grin on her face.

"Kill my husband?" she whispered as if there was someone other than me in the house.

"Yeah, secure the bag, sis." I took a couple of shots while Kadence rolled the shittiest blunt I had ever seen in my life.

"What about jail? I would never make it there." I handed her another shot.

"That's why you don't get caught." Kadence appeared to be actually considering it. She lit the blunt and passed it to me.

"I'm tired of being a dummy. Something has got to give." I filled my lungs with the smoke and blew it in Kadence's direction.

"Loyal is always MIA. Make him disappear when no one is expecting him to be around. You watch all that crazy people shit on the ID channel. Take some notes and make it happen." She hit the blunt and started coughing immediately.

"Does Bryson have a gun?"

"Bitch! You will not implicate my man in this. I can get you one though. Are you sure about this?" Kadence nodded her head.

"What other option is there?" She poured another shot and stood up. "I got to pee. I'll be back." She stumbled up the hall to the bathroom.

A few minutes later, Kadence returned with a sad look on her face.

"Are you gonna be okay, Kadence?" She nodded her head.

"Yeah, I have to get home to my daughter."

I watched her struggle to get her keys out of her purse. Kadence was leaning. There was no way I could let her drive home in that condition. She was still struggling when the doorbell rang. Ashlee stepped inside with a smile on her face.

"Whassup ladies."

"Hey, Ash." She closed the door behind her.

"What y'all up to?" Kadence was the first to speak, loudly.

"I'm bout to go kill my husband." Ashlee looked at Kadence and then at me.

"You gone poison him?" she said with a sparkle in her eye. "That's how I killed my last husband," Ashlee whispered with a huge grin. I couldn't tell if she was joking or not, but Kadence was all ears.

"Come in, have a seat with us," her words slurred, and she forgot that she was just on her way out the door. Ashlee and I did our exchange as Kadence poured her a shot. She shoved the shot glass at Ashlee. "So, what did you use?"

"Well, he was sick and already on a bunch of medications. I just increased the dosage a little more each day. He died one night while he was sleeping."

"That's it?" Kadence looked disappointed. "So you ain't do no gangsta shit?" Ashlee shook her head and laughed aloud.

"No baby, gangsta shit gets you caught, and I got too much to lose." Kadence nodded her head.

"You're right." I could still see the wheels turning in her head. Ashlee passed the blunt to Kadence.

"But, I will tell you this though. Getting rid of the body will be the hardest part. You have to be careful not to leave any kind of evidence behind. If you're gonna draw blood, do it in a place where it can go unnoticed. Being messy will have your ass looking like them hoes on Orange is the Black, and I know you don't want that." Kadence was on the edge of her seat, hanging on to every word that came from Ashlee's mouth.

"What if I can't move him?"

"You need a team of people you can trust to keep their damn mouths shut. Some people will sell you out for a dime bag of loud. Trust me, I know."

"Well, you know I got you in whatever you decide to do." Kadence smiled, and as quickly as she started smiling, she was crying.

"I don't understand why he won't just act right!" she cried. Ashlee handed her a tissue off the table next to her.

"Because he's a man, baby. Men don't know how to act right. It's like it's something programmed in their DNA to do the exact opposite of what they're asked. You say be faithful, and he takes that as smash every bitch you see." Ashlee chuckled, downing another shot. "If you don't mind me asking, who is your husband?"

"Loyal Jackson," Kadence said quickly forgetting that she didn't know this damn woman from a can of paint. Hell, I barely knew her, and she had been my supplier for almost five years.

"Girl! You talking about killing Loyal? Let me sing to you Loyal?" Kadence's smile faded.

"He said that to you?" Ashlee rolled another blunt and put it in the air.

"No, he's not my type. But, I do have a couple of friends he used that weak ass line with." Kadence stared at Ashlee.

"I have to go home." She stood and stumbled out the door. Ashlee looked confused.

"Did I say something wrong? I poured another shot and shook my head.

"No, she knows her nigga ain't shit." I stared at Ashlee who was smiling. For the first time, I realized how pretty she was. I guess I stared a little too long because her words brought me back to reality.

"I don't like girls," she said quickly. I looked around the room trying to figure out what gave her the impression that I did.

"Um... okay?" She smiled and changed the subject. I was starting to wonder if I gave off some kind of lesbian vibe. Everyone questioned my sexuality lately.

"Is she really going to kill Loyal?" Ashlee changed the subject.

"Naw, Kadence is in her feelings and talking shit. She won't leave him let alone kill him."

Ashlee and I sat there talking for hours before I got that damn text from Loyal begging me to meet him. Kadence never mentioned killing her husband again, but I had a feeling it stayed in the back of her mind.

WHEN I FINALLY MADE IT home, the first thing I wanted to do is take a shower. I ran my bath water then took off my clothes and threw them into the washing machine with some peroxide to remove any blood that was there. I hated coming home to this empty house. The bath that was supposed to relax me had me even more on edge. I washed my body and climbed into bed. The silence was killing me. I turned on the TV. The new episode of *Power* was just about to start, and I had to watch it now before everybody on social media ruined the fuckin' episode. I made myself comfortable while Joe sang my favorite introduction song. I picked up my phone and realized I had no one to call. I went to Facebook as I often did when I was bored. I saw thousands of people wishing Kadence well and cursing Loyal's name.

"If only y'all knew."

I got out of bed and popped two Xanies. Sleep would have to come one way or another. I rolled a blunt and got back in bed, anxious for the day to be over with.

3

KENEDEE

I pulled into Kadence's driveway at the same time that the cleaning crew pulled up. I got out the car and met them on the sidewalk.

"My sister was shot here about a week ago, and I don't want her to have to come home and see this. Do whatever you have to do to get rid of all the blood."

"Yes, ma'am." The man followed me into the house. I turned and waited for his reaction. He smiled and nodded his head.

"I can handle this for you, ma'am. You said about a week ago?" He stared at the huge stain on the rug. A small spot was a little brighter than the rest of the dark-stained carpet.

"Yeah, give or take a few days." I flashed my best smile and twirled my hair around my finger.

"Okay, no problem." I walked away and started opening the windows to let the smell out of the house. My phone started to ring. "*Unknown caller*" flashed on the screen. I pressed ignore, not really in the mood for the bullshit. However, the caller was persistent. In less than a minute, there were five missed calls. I answered the next one with an attitude.

"Who the hell is this?"

"Baby girl, I missed you. Please don't hang up." I rolled my eyes and walked up the stairs. Kyle had been calling me nonstop since I found out that he had been having Paris fuckin' stalk me.

"Why are you calling?" I sat on Kadence's bed. Her room was just the way she left it. It even still smelled like the perfume she always wore.

"I need to see you, Kenedee."

"You need to be with your wife." He let out a loud sigh.

"Where are you? Are you at Kadence's? I can be there in five minutes." I got up and looked out the window.

"Why are you five minutes away from her house? You don't even live over there."

"I need to see you, Kenedee. Stop with the games."

"Kyle, it is over between us. Your wife tries to kill me every time you come around. Stay the fuck away from me. You bring danger with you." I hung up the phone just as Kyle's car parked in front of the cleaning van.

"Oh my God what is he doing here?" I ran down the stairs. I stopped in the foyer because there was four men steam cleaning the carpet.

"Hey, guys do me a favor?" The man who I assumed to be the supervisor of the group looked up at me and smiled.

"What's that, baby girl?" The sound of those two words together almost made me throw up.

"Actually, two favors. One, don't ever call me that again. And two, there is a gentleman outside, please don't let him in. Don't let anyone in."

"Anything you say, beautiful." I rolled my eyes and went back upstairs.

My phone kept vibrating in my hand until I turned the power off completely. Kyle was still sitting in his car. I hoped that eventually, he would get the hint. It was over between us. After all the shit that my sister had just gone through, I never wanted to mess with someone else's husband. Hell, I barely even wanted my own at this point. These niggas were out here losing their damn minds and lives over pussy. I couldn't understand it at all. My life was way more valuable than what I had between my legs. The shit was fun while it lasted, but too much had happened, and I needed to be there for my sister. Not bring more heat into her life.

I laid across the California king-sized bed. I didn't know what was going to happen to Loyal, but I hoped he would rot in that damn cell for what he did to Kadence. I thought about Kai who hadn't even asked about her father. She was used to him not being around and this was nothing unusual for her. I peeked in his nightstand to see what he had stashed inside. Just like I hoped, there was a bag of weed and a pack of cones. I filled the cone and laid back in the bed. The 60-inch TV covered the wall in front of the bed. I turned it to VH1. I was in love with rachet television. I could watch it all day. It gave me a break from reality. I was halfway done when there was a knock at the door.

"Hang on a second." I put the cone in the ashtray next to the bed and ran to the door.

"Ma'am, I wanted you to come and take a look at the carpet. See if you'd rather just replace it all together." I pulled the door closed behind me and followed him out to the foyer. The door was open just enough for the thick cord to run out to the truck. The stain was almost gone but not enough.

"Is that all that will come up?" I looked him up and down for the first time, noticing his name tag. Zane took off his hat and smiled at me.

"I could stay longer if you like, but I have to send my crew to another job. I can't promise that it will get much better than this because it set for so long." I thought about it for a second.

"Do you install carpet?" He shook his head.

"I usually don't, but I could make an exception for you." He smiled again showing off his dimples this time. "I admire what you're doing for your sister. Nobody should have to walk into this type of reminder." They had cleaned up most of the mess, and it almost looked normal in there. I opened my mouth to speak, but the front door opened. Kyle walked in looking like he hadn't washed his ass in weeks.

"You just turn your phone off? I tell you I'm outside and you turn your phone off?" Kyle yelled, moving closer to me. .

"What the hell are you doing, Kyle?" Zane looked back forth between the two of us.

"I said I needed to see you." He took a step closer. Zane started to move out of the way, and I stopped him.

"You can't be here. I'm busy, and you're married, so goodbye." Kyle focused in on Zane.

"Really Kenedee? You're stunting on me for the help?" Zane pushed me behind him and took a step closer to Kyle.

"My mans, she asked you to leave."

Kyle charged at Zane who stepped to the side and pulled me with him. Kyle fell flat on his face in the spot that Zane and his few had been cleaning.

"Kenedee, baby girl, I just want to talk to you."

"Kyle, you need to get the fuck out."

Zane helped him to his feet and pushed him out the door. Kyle slumped back to his car a broken man. I just knew his feelings were hurt. Zane stood in the doorway until Kyle pulled off and the turned back to me.

"You must have put it on him." He shook his head and laughed.

"But he got a whole ass wife though! Why do men do that?" Zane licked his lips.

"Maybe you ain't been messing with the right ones." I looked down at his ring finger with no sign of a wedding band. I know I just said I would take it slow with men, but my pussy was saying otherwise.

"Maybe, but back to what we should be discussing." I walked in front of him and bent over to inspect the carpet. I could literally feel him staring "How long would it take you to replace this? My sister could be home at any moment now." He pulled out his phone.

"Let me find the right carpet and then we will go from there." I motioned for him to follow me.

"You can sit in here. Can I get you anything?"

"No ma'am." I shook my head and sat down on the table in front of him.

"My name is Kenedee. Everyone calls me Ken."

"Nice to meet you, Ken. I'm Zane." Zane was fine! I mean drop everything and bust it open fine.

From the way he spoke to the way he walked, everything about him was sexy as hell. He looked up from his phone and caught me staring.

"So aside from the stalker cat, are you single, Ms. Ken?" I climbed off the table and smiled. I was happy to finally have his attention.

"As a dollar bill. What about you? Any lucky ladies have a piece of your heart?" Zane laughed.

"Ladies? As in more than one? What kind of man do you think I am?" I felt my face turning red.

"I didn't mean it like that. I just meant—" He raised his hand to prevent me from further putting my foot in my mouth.

"I was married; my wife died a couple of years ago." He stared at me with his big brown eyes. "She got in a car accident. A drunk driver ran her off the road, and she died right there." I walked over and sat down at the table beside him.

"I'm so sorry to hear that." Zane nodded his head.

"It was hard at first. We had been together since high school. It gets easier every day though."

I sat there hanging on to his every word. I don't know what it was, but I was intrigued. He excused himself to answer his phone, and I realized that mine was still powered off. I ran upstairs to get it. As soon as it was on, messages and Facebook alerts started coming through. I had a few from Bryson. I dialed his number back.

"Hey, I'm here at the house now. Where are y'all at?" Bryson cleared his throat.

"I got us a room. You're cleaning it up now?"

"Yeah, I hired a cleaning crew. It was too much for me to do alone. They got the majority of it up, but there's still a stain. Now we're trying to find the right carpet to replace it." Bryson was quiet, so quiet that I thought he had hung up on me. "You still there?"

"Yeah, I'm here. Just tell them to send me the bill. If you can't find the carpet, pick out some tile your sister would like. I don't think she'll care."

"Okay. Make sure you get some rest. Tell Kadence I love her, and I'll be over to see her when everything is squared away here."

"Okay. See you later." He hung up fast. I walked back down the stairs where Zane was waiting for me.

"I think I found the right one. You want to ride with me to get it?" I nodded my head, running down the stairs. I stopped when I got outside.

"You wanna take my car?" I pointed to my bright red Camaro shining in the sun.

"Your car is too small. You got a problem with my van?" Normally I would mind, but something about him made it okay.

"No, the van in fine." I tucked my keys into my purse. After making sure, I had my pepper spray handy I climbed in Zane's work van. He turned on the radio, and some 90s R&B singer cried about how he needed to find love.

"I like you, Kenedee. I think we could have a lot of fun together." I looked up at him and smiled.

"Well, let's find out." I sat back in the seat while Zane drove in the after-work traffic.

4

BRYSON

I would be lying if I said a part of me wasn't turned on seeing Kadence blow that punk nigga's brains out. The other part was nervous though. I didn't know what to believe. Did she ever have amnesia? Was all of this a part of their plan? Her fucking me and getting knocked up. I had so many questions, but all I could do was wait until she came back. I sat out on the patio with my blunt and waited. All this time I thought Kadence was a softee. I guess it was true that every person had a breaking point. I had spent years watching her letting motherfuckas run her over and then crying about it. I had just finished the blunt when my cell started to ring.

"Whassup baby?" I was anxious to see Kadence. I felt like a bitch, my stomach was in knots, and my heart was beating fast just seeing her name on my caller ID.

"Hey, I'm down in the lobby. What room are you in?"

"417," I said quickly opening the door for her to come inside. I laid across the bed and listened as she got in the elevator and made her way to me. A few seconds later she pushed open the door with a smile on her face. All the questions I had faded away when I had her standing in front of me. Kadence was glowing. She had a huge grin on her face as she walked closer to the bed.

"Are you mad at me?" she whispered, climbing on top of me.

"Naw, but we gone talk." Kadence smiled and leaned down to kiss me. My dick grew underneath her soft but firm body.

"I've missed you, Bryson." I flipped her over so that I was on top.

"I was so worried about you, baby. Don't do no shit like that again."

I pulled her dress over her head and kissed her from head to toe. Kadence squirmed with each kiss. I pulled her panties down and threw them across the room. Kadence spread her legs, and I kissed all over her pussy. Kadence moaned and slid into a sitting position. I wrapped my arms around her legs and pulled her back down.

"Ain't no point in running baby, you gone bust regardless." I slurped on her pussy, writing our names on her clit with my tongue.

"Oh my god!" Kadence was screaming, making me feel like I was doing the damn thing. Her body stiffened, and she came all over my face, but I couldn't stop. She tasted so good, and when you finally get the girl that you've been dreaming about smashing, you don't want that shit to end.

"Bryson, babe, please stop." She pushed at my head, but I wasn't budging. She was back in a sitting position. Her back was arched, and she was begging for me to stop making her come.

"You want me to stop for real?" I paused, flicking my tongue back and forth over her clit.

"I don't know," she moaned quietly.

I took that as a no and dove back in. She had her fingers wrapped in my dreads and pulled me closer. I laughed and sucked that motherfucka dry. When Kadence looked like she couldn't take anymore, I stepped out of my clothes and rubbed the head of my dick and down her clit. I grabbed her legs and pulled them until she was lying down and each of her long legs rested on my shoulder.

"Stop teasing me."

I looked down at Kadence, and she was beautiful. I didn't know what I did to deserve her, but I was grateful. I closed my eyes and slid inside. She felt better than I remembered. I was glad I made her come so hard before because I ain't know how long I would last. I focused on the TV. I watched as zombies chased the last few humans on earth. Kadence moaned and wrapped her arms around my neck and pulled me closer to her. She moaned in my ear and kissed me passionately. I lost all control and bust inside her. I rolled beside her and wrapped my arms around her.

"I'm glad you're back." I kissed her on the forehead.

"Me too." Since I had busted a nut, I was thinking more clearly.

"So tell me whassup?" Kadence pushed herself into a sitting position.

"What do you wanna know?"

"Everything." I walked to the bathroom, washed my dick and wet a towel for Kadence. "I'm listening."

"A few months ago I got the idea for Jazelle and a friend of hers. I thought about it, but not seriously until I caught him and Jazelle together."

"Jazelle and Loyal fuckin' wasn't a part of the plan?" I started rolling up while she talked.

"She said when I finally got tired that I would end it. I didn't know anything about their relationship until that night. Me hooking up with you was me acting on pure emotions, but Jazzy was right though. That night after I left you, I knew I was done. I knew I would kill Loyal I just needed the perfect opportunity. I already knew how he felt about you and me, so I used that to my advantage. I expected him to want to fight, and I figured I could say it was self-defense. The gun surprised me. After he shot me and I survived, I knew he had to die."

"And the amnesia?" Kadence cleared her throat.

"For the first few days, it was real. Then little memories started to come back, with everything I heard on the news. I didn't fully remember until I saw the two of them together. When I heard you and Kenedee talking about the house being cleaned, I saw that as an opportunity. When you went to the bathroom, I texted Jazelle to bail Loyal out, which she did, no questions asked. I knew Loyal would try to run because he's not a jail type of nigga. If he had the chance to be free, he would take it. There were about 15 stacks in the safe in our bedroom, and he needed that to start out."

I was smoking my blunt amazed by how sneaky she actually was. I mean who the fuck faked having amnesia. A sneaky motherfucka is who.

"Was Kenedee in on this?" Kadence shook her head.

"No, Kenedee is a blabbermouth. She would have never been able to keep the secret. I'm just lucky to have sisters who love me and would do anything for me. When Ken said that she would clean the place that really meant she would hire someone. That's why I suggested we should go home. If I timed everything right, we would all be there at the same time. I was just lucky Kenedee hadn't made it there." She stood up and walked over to the bathroom. Kadence leaned against the door before going inside.

"When I walked in and saw all that blood and then Loyal and Jazelle, I just lost it. I didn't want you to be able to snatch what I had been planning for so long, so I took my shot."

My dick was getting hard hearing her explain everything. Call me crazy, but this was the kind of girl you needed on your team, as long as you stay on her good side.

"It may not seem like it, but I peep everything. I studied my family to the point that I had this shit down to a science. My mama always said you gotta stay one step ahead of everybody, if you don't wanna get left behind." Kadence smiled at me. "I have to use the bathroom."

She disappeared into the bathroom. I laid down and tried to absorb everything that Kadence had just dropped on me. It made me love her even more. She peeked her head around the corner and poked her bottom lip out.

"I'm sorry I lied to you." I got up and walked over to her. I turned on the shower on and pulled her under the water with me.

"Let that be the last motherfuckin' time." I pushed her up against the wall and kissed her. I planned to keep Kadence close to me, mainly because I didn't know what letting her go would mean for me.

After our second round in the shower, Kadence laid across the bed while I got dressed.

"Kenedee is at the house with the cleaners now. She says they're going to replace the whole floor in the front hallway." She nodded her head with her eyes partially closed. "I got a few errands to run. You need anything?"

"Hot wings and Sprite," she mumbled while getting more comfortable on the bed.

I walked out the room, feeling like a new man. All that time spent in the hospital had me feeling like a chump. As soon as I made it down to my truck, my phone started to ring. I ignored the call and made my way back to my old neighborhood. I rarely came home, and when I did, it was because I needed information.

I pulled up in front of my mother's bright pink house. Nothing had changed. My older brother still sat on the porch with music blasting from the front window. The smell of fried chicken filled the block as soon as I stepped outside my truck.

"Whassup, lil' bro'?" Braylon stood to greet me.

"I can't call it. What's been going on around here?" Braylon took a seat on the faded rocking chair that had been there for as long as I could remember.

"Same shit, different day." I nodded my head. Braylon was the definition of a mama's boy. At damn near 40, he had yet to move from the room we shared growing up.

"Mama's in there?" Braylon nodded his head. "Bruce is too." I ignored his last comment.

Bruce was the youngest of the three of us, and the most irresponsible. I only heard from him when he needed to be bailed out of jail. The last time I couldn't get there in time, and he disowned me. As far as I was concerned, my moms had two sons and a leech. I walked in and followed the smell of the chicken.

"Hey, mama." I kissed her cheek and grabbed a piece of chicken from the stove.

"Well, look who finally found their way home. I thought you forgot about us little people." She handed me a napkin. "And I hope your hands are clean."

"They clean, mama." I held my hands up as if that could prove anything. She frowned her face and began making me a plate.

"How is Jazelle." So much had happened so fast, I hadn't had a chance to tell her about the changes in our relationship.

"Jazelle is good, but we're not together anymore." It seemed like my mama wore a permanent frown whenever I was talking to her.

"What did she do?"

"That's not important. How are you doing?" She sat the plate of baked macaroni and cheese, collard greens, sweet potatoes and hot water cornbread in front of me.

"I'm alive." The same response she always gave. "Since you're single I know you're not eating good. Let me make you a plate to take home." I cleared my throat.

"Could you make one for Kadence too?" Mama put her hand over her heart.

"Oh my god! How is Kadence? I saw what happened to her on the news. I always knew that Loyal was no good. Didn't I tell you that?" I nodded my head. The munchies had set in and finishing this plate was my primary focus. "Bless her poor little heart."

"Kadence is good, ma. She's recovering fast, better than any of us expected." Mama looked at me like she wanted to say more, but Bruce walked in the room.

"Mama! Did you make my plate? I gotta pick Irish up, and you know how she gets when I'm late." I slid my chair away from the table and stood to walk out. Mama stood in front of me.

"Your brother is here, Bruce. I didn't hear either one of you speak. I know I raised you both better." She put her hands on her hips and stared back and forth between the two of us. Bruce poked out his bottom lip and stood in front of me.

"Whassup nigga?" I stared him down, debating on if I wanted to listen to my mama or not.

"Whassup?" I pulled my little brother into a hug. "Is life treating you, right?"

Bruce nodded his head, sitting down at the table with his plate. I kissed my mama on her cheek, grabbed Kadence's plate, and went back outside. I walked out to my truck motioning for Braylon to follow me. He walked down the stairs with a cigarette hanging from his bottom lip.

"What's good youngin'?" He climbed in the truck, dropping the cigarette on the curb behind him.

"You know anything about a lady stick up kid?" Braylon frowned his face.

"A lady? You mean it's girls out here robbing niggas?" Braylon laughed loudly.

"That's what I heard. How's business going for you?" I stared at Braylon to see if he would tell me the truth.

Before I left home, Braylon and I had hit a lick that would have us set for life, if we handled it right. Braylon was street smart, but I had more common knowledge. I was smart enough to know what we had come up on, but also smart enough to know not to fuck around with it. We got over 100 kilos of cocaine and almost 3 million dollars. We split it in half. Braylon kept his half, while I sold mine and invested the money. All niggas from the hood weren't thugs. I had two beauty supply stores, a laundromat, and part in a local grocery store. Nobody knew because I moved quietly. Nobody needed to know. My main focus was making sure Kadence gave birth to a healthy baby and got out of whatever game she and Jazelle had been playing for so many years.

"Business is business; nothing you need to worry about, lil' bro. I got this." Braylon avoided looking me in my eyes. I knew something was going on, but I didn't press the issue. He handed me a small envelope. "Clean this for me?"

I nodded my head and slid the envelope into my pocket. "It'll be in the bank next week." Braylon nodded his head and started to get out.

"Aye, let me know if you hear about any moves being made by them."

Braylon nodded his head and walked back to his usual spot on the porch. I drove to the store and got Kadence her Sprite. I don't know what she had done to me, but any amount of time was too much away from her.

5

JAZELLE

I woke up to the sound of my doorbell ringing. I looked over at my alarm clock. It was 2:15 in the damn morning! I grabbed my hot pink robe from the edge of the bed and walked to the door. I could see the flashing lights before I even opened the door. A huge lump started to form in my throat. I knew they would come, but I thought I had more time. I opened the door, rubbing imaginary sleep from my eyes.

"Yes?"

"Sorry to bother you so late ma'am. Are you the owner of a 2016 Lincoln LS?" I nodded my head.

"Yes, is there a problem?" The younger officer smiled.

"Ma'am, you might want to get dressed. We need to talk to you." I walked back to my bedroom and threw on a pair of sweats and a tank top. I had never been arrested before, but I knew better than to wear anything I wanted to see again. I took my time walking down the stairs. Both officers were dressed in their uniforms. I stared them both down.

"Am I under arrest?" The older officer, Officer Layne smiled.

"No, ma'am. We just want to ask you some questions."

I followed them out to their squad car. Neither one of them said anything, which left time for my mind to wonder. I hoped Kadence would come through like we planned. When I got the text to bail Loyal out, I didn't question it. Honestly, I was just excited she was talking to me again. I loved my sister with everything I had in me. I only wanted to make her life better. I know a lot of y'all think that I am the worst person in the world, but I did what I needed to do for my sister to come to her senses. Loyal cheating on her would have never made Kadence snap the way that she did. However, Loyal cheating with someone so close to her? That was the straw the broke the camel's back. I knew that Kadence would look for Loyal at the Sheraton. Cheaters always went to the place that they were most comfortable.

What I didn't plan was for her to lose her shit the way that she did. I was expecting her to be hurt and maybe even cry a little. But baby, when I say she demolished that damn room. The hotel staff kicked us out immediately. Superstar or not, Loyal had made the ultimate fuck up. I could tell by the look in Kadence's eyes that it was time. Having her hate me, made things difficult, but not much. I knew when she told me to bail him out shit was about to get real. I never bought that amnesia bullshit. I could tell by the way she looked at me that she knew who the fuck I was.

The squad car pulled up in front of the precinct. I stared at the building completely scared about what was about to happen. Officer Layne opened my door and led me into the station.

"Have a seat right here, Ms. Green." He motioned for me to sit in a lime green hard-plastic chair that looks like I would catch something just being close to it. I sat down and looked around the precinct.

There were a lot of police sitting around eating donuts. I fought to keep myself from laughing. I thought that shit was just something they said for TV. I looked down the long hallway, and my heart skipped a beat. Kadence and Kai were walking up the hall. Kadence looked at me and winked. I winked back and smiled at Kai. She had been through so much for such a little girl. I said a silent prayer for my niece. They were ushered into a room, and the door closed behind them. A few seconds later, Officer Layne came back and led me to the room across from where Kadence and Kai were. I sat down, and he sat down across from me.

"Do you know where your car is, Ms. Green?" I shook my head.

"No, I let my brother-in-law use it earlier. He hasn't come back yet. Is something wrong?" I stared at him, careful not to let my nervousness through.

"Your brother-in-law?"

"Yes, Loyal. He said he had to make some runs, and he couldn't get to his car, so I gave him my keys."

"Did he say what type of runs?" I shifted in my seat.

"I mean, I wasn't all in his business or anything. He just said runs." Officer Layne nodded his head and stared at the two-way mirror behind me. He slowly nodded his head.

"Ms. Green, Loyal Jackson's dead body was found in the trunk of your car a while ago. Do you have any idea how this could have happened?" I swallowed hard and at him.

"Loyal is dead? Have you all told my sister? What happened to him? I need to check on my sister." I went into a frenzy, being extra as hell. I forced tears from my eyes. Another officer, Officer Galloway walked in and sat down next to Officer Layne.

"Ms. Green, We know that you bailed Mr. Jackson from jail a few hours before he was found stuffed in the trunk of your vehicle. We also know that he had just shot your sister, now I'mma ask you again, do you know how any of this happened?" I looked back and forth between the two officers.

"I don't know anything. And why the hell would I waste all that money bailing that nigga out, just to kill him?" I sat back and stared at them. Neither one of them said a thing. Officer Galloway was the first to speak.

"What about the affair the two of you were having?" I cocked my head to the side and sucked my teeth.

"First off, it wasn't an affair. The whole thing got blown out of context." Officer Layne smiled. I didn't see shit funny, but I knew losing my cool would have my ass wearing an orange jumpsuit. He slammed his hands on the table so hard I thought the raggedy piece of shit would break in half.

"I'mma just ask the question, that's on everyone's mind. Did your sister put you up to this?"

"My sister? The one suffering from amnesia?" Officer Galloway walked over and hovered over me.

"Jazelle, we know the hell Loyal put your sister through. Do you expect us to believe y'all didn't want him gone?" I cleared my throat and crossed my arms over my chest.

"Am I under arrest? Because if I am, I need my lawyer. If I'm not, I would like to go home." There was a knock on the mirror behind me. Officer Galloway smiled.

"Ok Ms. Green, you are free to go." I stood and waited for them to open the door.

"How am I supposed to get home? I mean y'all did bring me here." As soon as I finished my sentence, the door opened, and a very distraught Kadence stepped out. I ran to her side, and Kai collapsed in my arms.

"Auntie Jazzy, somebody murdered my daddy!" she cried loudly, catching the attention of every person in the room.

"I'm so sorry, baby." I held her close to me as Kadence quietly dabbed the tears from her eyes.

"Let's get her out of here," Kadence whispered. She handed me the keys to her car. We walked to the car in silence. As soon as we pulled away from the station, Kadence pulled out her phone:

"Hey we're on our way, we need to talk." I had no idea who she called. For some reason, I felt like I didn't know the person sitting next to me. Kadence pulled into Mama Lena's driveway. She turned and looked at Kai.

"You okay, baby girl?" Kai nodded her head and got out the car without another word. I waited for Kadence to back out of the driveway.

"This shit is eating her up you know that, right?"

"Kai is a strong girl. She'll be fine. I mean it really ain't that different from when Loyal was alive. He was a paycheck dad. The insurance check will cover that aspect." Kadence sounded so cold and so different from her usual bubbly self.

"What about you? You okay?" She looked at me, and then quickly back at the road.

"What you mean?"

"Bitch, when the fuck was you gonna let me in on the plan?" Kadence smiled as she drove through traffic.

"It's the same plan, Jazzy. Did you forget?" I sat back in my seat and shook my head.

Kadence pulled up in front of Ashlee's house. I didn't even know them bitches knew each other. We got out the driveway and knocked on the door. Ashlee opened the door and motioned for us to follow her. A little boy stood in the middle of the hallway watching us as we walked by. He looked like the boy version of his mom. I wondered what he was doing up at this time of night, but it wasn't my business.

"Hey, ladies, what's up?" Ashlee bounced down on the couch and smiled at us.

"The police brought us both in this evening." Kadence sat down with a serious look on her face. Ashlee spit out her coffee, even though it was barely five in the morning.

"Did the insurance company contact you yet?" Kadence shook her head.

"No, just the police and as far as they're concerned, I still have amnesia." She turned and looked at me.

"And what about you?" I looked up and both of them were staring at me.

"I told them I let Loyal borrow my car, and I didn't know what he was up to." Ashlee burst into laughter.

"So, y'all bitches really about that life, huh? Taking niggas out one at a time!" The fact that she found this situation funny kind of bothered me, but not more than the fact that Kadence was putting so much trust into a person she barely bought weed from. Ashlee left the room and came back with a suitcase.

"Everything that you will need is in here. I'll put it where we discussed in the morning." Kadence handed Ashlee an envelope and walked towards the door.

"You need anything, sis?" Ashlee asked as I followed behind Kadence.

"Naw. I'll holla at you later though." As soon as we were out of Ashlee earshot, I stared at Kadence waiting for her to acknowledge me.

"Why do you keep staring at me, Jazelle? You got something to say to me?"

"What the fuck is going on? What's in the suitcase?"

"You know what you need to know right now Jazelle. You may fold under pressure. I can't tell you too much. You know your role, now play it."

I felt a little insulted, but I decided not to press the issue. There was a time and place for everything. Right now my main concern was keeping my ass out of jail. Kadence had shown me that she was not the person that I thought she was. That bitch switched up way too easily. I changed the subject.

"So, when are you due?"

"October 13th."

"I hope it's a boy," I said way too loud. Kadence gave me the side eye but said nothing. We drove the rest of the way in silence. She pulled into my driveway and put the car in park.

"Jazelle, you know I love you, right?" I nodded my head.

"Of course. Through thick and thin no matter what."

"Just stay focused okay? Don't let this baby distract you." I opened the door and got out.

"Your baby doesn't faze me, Kadence. I already knew what it was." I closed the door and walked away. That bitch had her fucking nerve!

6

KENEDEE

I sat on the stairs watching Zane lay the tile in Kadence's house.

"So, what do you do for fun?" I asked him, twirling my curls around my finger.

"I go to work; I don't have much time for fun. Money is more important." He stood up and admired his handy work. "What do you think?" I got up and stood next to him.

"This is nice. You can't even tell what went down here." Zane licked his lips and smiled at me.

"I aim to please." I had never been one to go for a blue-collar nigga, but it was something about this one that I couldn't let go.

"What are you about to do?" Zane looked down at his watch and laughed.

"I'm going to bed. I had been with you all day, woman." I laughed too.

"I guess I could let you go home." I opened the door as Zane packed up his equipment.

"But, I could take you to lunch." He paused and flashed that smile again.

I put my number in his phone as he promised to call me later. I closed and locked the door. I walked around the house, checking all of the locks on the doors and windows. I sent a text to Bryson to let him know that everything was cleared for Kadence to come back home. I sent a text to Kadence to let her know that I loved her and I would see her tomorrow. I laid down in the bed and turned on the TV. *Love & Hip Hop: Atlanta* was just starting, and it was my favorite show. There was something about watching other people go through drama, and it had nothing to do with you. I grabbed the blunt I was smoking earlier and lit it. My phone vibrated with a Facebook alert that Paris had tagged me in a post.

What the fuck is this bitch up too? I clicked on the notification and waited for the picture to load. It was one of us when we had first started classes at UW before all the weird shit went down. The caption read, *thinking about the old days.* I liked the post and then sat the phone down on the bed. I turned the TV up, and the phone started to ring as if whoever was calling knew that I was trying to hear it. Whoever was calling was not programmed in my phone, and I had half a mind to ignore it.

"What?"

"Hey Kenedee, how are you?" the familiar voice spoke loudly through the phone.

"Hey, um, what are you doing?" I wanted to ask why she was calling, but I decided to play nice for the moment.

"I just wanted to check on you." It was funny how Paris and Kyle just randomly wanted to check on me on the same day.

"I'm alive. But let me call you later, I gotta fix the TV." I quickly hung up the phone before she could say anything else. Everything about Paris creeped me the fuck out.

I got up and looked out the window just to make sure she or her psychotic ass uncle weren't camped outside. I tried to lay down, but I couldn't stop thinking that I was being watched by someone. I grabbed my purse and drove to my mama's house.

Even though it was the middle of the night, mama was up watching her infomercials like they were prime time television.

"Kenedee? Is everything okay?" I nodded my head and curled up on the couch.

"Kadence's place is all cleaned and ready for her to come home." Mama stood and walked into the kitchen. She came back with a glass of lemonade and some Tylenol.

"I'm so proud of the way you have had your sister's back during all this nonsense. She really needed you."

"I'mma always have my sister's back, ain't no way around it." Mama nodded her head.

"I just hope her memory comes back. *Lord, please watch over my child in her time of need,*" mama prayed loudly.

"She'll be fine. Kadence is too stubborn to not be fine. I just hope Loyal's ass gets what he deserves." Mama popped me on the side of my head.

"Watch your mouth."

"I'm sorry mama, but you can sit here and act like you're not pissed at Loyal for all the shit- I mean stuff he did to Kadence." Mama frowned and went back to her recliner.

"Karma has a way of coming back to those who deserve it. That's not for you or me to worry about." She turned the TV up and put her feet up.

"Mama, why are you not in bed?" I stood and walked over to help her back out of her chair.

"Kenedee, mind your damn business! You are worried about the wrong shit!" I held back my laughter and raised my hands in the air.

"My bad mama. I'm going to lay down. Wake me up if Kadence comes over."

I went to the guest bedroom and looked in on Kai. She was curled up holding her teddy bear. I covered her with a blanket I knew would end up on the floor in a matter of minutes. I plugged in her tablet and laid it on the nightstand. As much as she was on that damn thing, she never charged it. When I came back out in the hall, mama was already snoring. I went to her room and crawled in the bed. There was no point in both of us being uncomfortable.

～

THE NEXT MORNING, I woke up to Kai climbing in bed with me.

"Good morning, TT Ken."

"Morning baby, how are you feeling?"

"Sad," she whispered before she burst into tears. I sat up and wrapped her arms around her.

"Aw Kai, calm down. Your mom is fine." I stroked her hair. She was crying uncontrollably, and I had no idea what to do.

"My mom will, but daddy will never be okay," she cried. As much as I hated Loyal, seeing my niece cry broke my heart.

"I'm sure your daddy will be fine too. He'll probably call you in a few hours." She looked up at me. Kai wiped the snot from her nose with the back of her hand.

"My daddy is dead, TT Ken." I stared at Kai thinking I must have heard her incorrectly.

"Maaaaa!" I yelled. Within seconds, mama was standing in the doorway. "What is she talking about? She said Loyal is dead?" Mama looked at Kai, and she repeated herself.

"I overheard the police talking to my mama at the hotel. They said that my daddy was found in the trunk of a car," Kai managed to get out in between sobs.

Mama pulled her phone from the pocket of her housecoat. She turned and walked up the hallway, but I could hear her saying. "What the fuck is going on, Bryson?"

I wrapped my arms around Kai and led her into the living room. Mama was pacing the floor, with the phone pressed to her ear. He face was pissed, but her voice was soft.

"Why didn't anyone tell us? Kai just broke down, and Kenedee and I had no idea what her problem was."

Kai was in my arms still crying. I searched for the words to comfort her, but I found none. Truth be told, I was relieved that Loyal was dead. He had been putting my sister through hell for years. Kai cried silently. Mama hung up the phone and stared at me. She walked over and pulled Kai into her arms.

"I'm sorry that you had to go through that! If your mother were in her right mind, she would have never taken you there." Kai wiped her face and stared at mama.

"Did my daddy hurt my mommy?" We exchanged glances. Mama slowly nodded her head.

"Now my mommy won't cry anymore then." Kai turned and walked up the hallway and into the bathroom.

"Should I go check on her?" I started up the hallway, but mama stopped me.

"Give her a minute. She'll be okay." Mama walked into the kitchen and started making breakfast.

I grabbed my purse off the table and went outside to smoke, which had become a regular habit of mine now. The sun was shining brightly. I shielded my eyes as a car sped around the corner so fast the tires squeaked. I put on my sunglasses just in time to see the back end of a Chevy Impala. I shook my head and called it a coincidence. I lit my blunt and leaned back on the porch swing. Shit was getting too out of hand for me. I was halfway finished with my blunt when Jazelle pulled up. She got out of the car and took her time walking up to the house. She had a huge teddy bear and a pink gift bag.

"Good morning, Ken. Is Kai awake?" I stared her down but said nothing.

Jazelle smacked her lips and continued in the house. As far as I was concerned, she died right along with Loyal. Both of them were a waste of fucking space. I got up and went in behind her to see what kind of lies she was feeling my mama's head with.

"They called me in for questioning too."

"Why would you be a suspect?" I jumped in the conversation. Jazelle looked at me and dropped her head. Mama sat down on the couch next to her and rubbed her back.

"Loyal was found in my trunk..."

"Wait a motherfuckin' minute! Why was Loyal in your trunk? How did he get with you?" I fired questions at Jazelle without giving her a chance to answer. She rolled her eyes at me.

"I bailed Loyal out." Mama snatched her hand away from Jazelle and stared with her mouth wide open.

"Bitch, are you fuckin' stupid? I smacked Jazelle as hard as I could. "What the fuck is wrong with you?" Mama jumped in between us.

"Kenedee! Relax!" Mama roared at me. I stopped across the room and sat down in the recliner.

"I hope Kadence kills yo' ass. I ain't ever heard of a fuck girl until I met you." Mama stood in front of me and spoke softly.

"Jazelle, baby, help me understand where your head is?" Jazelle was quiet.

"Make it make sense, bitch!" I yelled at her, clapping in between each word. I was two seconds off her ass, and mama wasn't going to be able to save her.

"I had to get him out. I had to know what the hell happened between them." I stood up and moved mama to the side.

"So, you team Loyal?" I asked, pulling my hair into a ball on the top of my head.

"There's some shit you don't understand, Kenedee." Jazelle stood to her feet and to me that meant she wanted to fight.

"I understand you got my sister fucked up!" I raised my fist to punch her and Bryson grabbed me from behind.

"Good morning." Kadence looked around confused. "Did we come at a bad time?" Bryson had a tight grip on me, while mama blocked Jazelle.

"Put me down, Bryson." I struggled to get free, but this nigga was strong as fuck! "I'm fine." I walked over and hugged Kadence.

"Good morning, sis. You need to drag this bitch!" I said and walked up the hall to check on Kai before I caught a case my damn self. Jazelle and I were gonna have our day. It was some shit that you just didn't do, and it seemed like this bitch needed a refresher.

7

KADENCE

I f I couldn't say anything else about Kenedee, I could say she rode for me to the highest degree, and that is why I forever had her back.

"What is going on?" I looked back and forth from mama to Jazelle. Neither of them wanted to speak up. "You guys are scaring me." Mama walked over and helped me over to the couch.

"How are you feeling today, Kadence? How's your memory?" I made myself comfortable on the couch and smiled at her.

"Little morning sickness, but I'm good. Some things are a little foggy, but I can remember a lot."

"Jazelle? Do you remember her?" I nodded my head.

"That's my big sister."

"Fuckin' traitor!" Kenedee yelled from another part of the house. I fought the urge to laugh. Kenedee had never liked Jazelle, and now she had lost filter completely. Low key, Jazelle deserved it. Since I was pregnant, I might as well let Kenedee tap that ass for me. Mama frowned.

"Is her mouth always that bad?" Mama nodded her head.

"Unfortunately, I heard you talked to the police last night. What did they say to you?" I cleared my throat and looked up at Bryson.

"They came to the hotel and told me that Loyal had been murdered. That they had found his body in the trunk of a car that had been driven into Lake Mendota. They wanted me to look at pictures and see if I recognized him as the man that had shot me."

"And was he?" I nodded my head. Kenedee had come back into the room and was standing in the doorway looking at me.

"Do you remember what happened the night you were shot?" Mama asked; her face was full of worry.

"A little. I remember watching TV with Bryson and Loyal blowing my phone up. I remember him showing up and demanding I stay away from Bryson, but that's all I remember." The look on my mama's face broke my heart. I knew she didn't want to believe that Loyal and I had come to this. She put her hand on my knee.

"What's cooking?" I asked, trying to change the subject. Mama smiled and helped me to my feet.

"I made all of your favorites. Sausage, bacon, home fries, cheese grits, biscuits, and eggs for Kenedee." I smiled and followed her to the kitchen.

"Mama, why did you make so much? Are you trying to make me fat?"

"You're eating for two now. That cute shit is over with." Mama pulled me over to the counter and handed me a plate.

"You think they know anything?" she whispered. I shook my head, while she loaded my plate with everything.

"No. Nobody knows anything." Kenedee walked in and grabbed a plate.

"Nobody knows what?"

"My due date yet." I headed to the table with my plate and started eating. Kenedee smiled. Her attitude had disappeared, and she just seemed happy to be around me. She sat down close to me, way too close.

"I hope it's a boy. I would love to go shopping for boy clothes instead of all this little girl shit. Kai is such a typical girl." She rolled her eyes and laughed. We ate breakfast and shared memories until Kenedee spoke up.

"You know Jazelle's in there with Bryson unsupervised? You better get in there." I looked to mama who was already on her way to the living room.

"Bryson! Get in here and get some breakfast." Kenedee and I laughed.

"Why are you so hard on her?"

"Because you never are! Jazelle has been jealous of you from jump. Everything you had, she needed parts in it. She acted like your friend and the first chance she got she fucked your husband. What's even worse is that she bailed the motherfucka out of jail after he tried to kill you. I don't know what kind of creepy shit she on, but she will never get no kind of love from me." Kenedee pounded on the table for emphasis. "If we weren't at Hogwarts, that bitch would be on slytherin."

"What?" Kenedee had lost me completely, as she often did when she was high.

"A fuckin' snake!" She moved her arm in a slithering motion. I couldn't contain my laughter as slid her arm in and out of my face.

"Kenedee. You are a fuckin' nut! I love you." She wrapped her arm around my neck and squeezed.

"I love you too, sis." Kenedee punched me in the arm. "And don't ever fuckin' scare me like that again! Comas and shit, who does that?" I rubbed my arm. Her lil' spoiled ass had some power behind them fists. I felt bad for keeping Kenedee out of the loop, but it was better that way.

"I'm sorry. Don't worry about me; you know I'm always good." I stood up and went to check on Kai. With everything that had been going on, I knew my daughter had to be heartbroken. I knocked on her door, and she didn't answer, so I left myself in.

"Kai? It's mommy, mind if I come in?" She sat up on the side of the bed. The look on my baby's face made me question everything that I had done. In my head, I was doing this to keep my daughter secured away from her no good daddy all while making sure she would be financially set for the rest of her life. But, what if I had actually caused more damage than good.

"Hey, mommy. How's your head?" I smiled and sat on the bed next to her.

"I'm fine, how are you?" She took a deep breath and laid back on the bed.

"I don't know how I feel." I laid next to her and propped myself up on my elbows.

"Wanna talk about it?" Kai looked at me. Her eyes wide and her lip poked out.

"Is it bad that I'm a little happy my daddy died?"

"Why are you happy?"

"Because he only made you cry. He was never really the best daddy; I only said that to make him feel better." She shrugged her shoulders. "But then, I kind of miss him. I wonder if he misses me, but I know he can't because he's dead."

"Well, it's okay to miss him. Even though he's gone, he's still your father. And, he wasn't always a bad guy."

"Then why did he shoot you and make you not remember anything?" As much as I hated to make excuses for Loyal's bitch ass, I didn't want my daughter happy that her father was gone. That was a lot of baggage for a little girl.

"Sometimes, people make mistakes. Remember when your broke mommy's glass?" Kai nodded her head.

"I didn't feel good, and I dropped it on accident."

"Exactly! Daddy wasn't feeling well. He didn't mean to shoot me; it was an accident."

"Auntie Ken doesn't think so." I chuckled.

"Well, we know Auntie Ken doesn't think anybody makes mistakes, does she?"

"If something happens, it's because it was meant to." We repeated Kenedee's motto together. Kai smiled and moved closer to me.

"Mommy?"

"Yes, baby?"

"Is Uncle Bryson gonna live with us now?"

"Do you think he should?" Kai was grinning like a kid on Christmas morning. She nodded her head rapidly.

"Uncle B is the best, for real mom. He always makes sure we're doing good, and he buys me an iPad every year!" Kai's excitement was catching.

"Maybe we'll keep him around a little longer then." I hugged Kai and pulled her to her feet. "Come get some breakfast; your granny made a bunch of stuff." Kai checked herself in the mirror, another sign she had been spending too much time with Kenedee.

When we got in the kitchen, Bryson and Kenedee were still eating. Mama was washing dishes, but Jazelle was nowhere to be found. I walked down to my old room and found Jazelle standing in front of the mirror holding a picture of Loyal and us a few weeks after the talent show.

"You remember this day?" She half smiled as she handed me the picture.

LOYAL *and I were about to the carnival that the school was having. I had asked if Jazelle could come along and after almost 30 minutes of pouting, Loyal was not budging.*

"Jazelle can't find her own man? Why she always got to go with us?" Loyal tossed his basketball up in the air.

"Because that's my best friend, Lonzell. She doesn't have any family here; you know that. Why does she bother you so much?"

"She's always cockblockin'! I'mma fuck around and have blue balls fuckin' with her." I fought back my laughter and walked over to Loyal.

"Just let her go this one time, I promise I'll make it worth your while." I leaned in and kissed him. Loyal pulled me closer to him and slid his hands underneath my shirt. Jazelle walked in without knocking.

"Hey, what are y'all up to?" Loyal bounced the ball so hard it smacked the ceiling before slowly bouncing under my desk.

"She's got a fuckin' lo jack on you." Loyal left my room, slamming the door behind him.

"What's his problem?"

"He's just horny. He'll be fine."

"Girl, you bet not let that man leave here horny. Ain't no tellin' what

bitch he will run into before he makes it back here." I pushed what Jazelle said out of my mind.

"Do you like anybody? Maybe we could double date or something. Jazelle pulled a joint from her purse and walked over to the window.

"Like anybody like who? These Wisconsin niggas are lame."

"Not all of them." I smiled and thought about my baby.

"Yeah, you got lucky." If I didn't know any better, I would have thought that there was a little jealousy in her voice.

"Don't worry. We'll find you somebody." I wrapped my arm around her shoulder. Jazelle swiped my arm away and blew a cloud of smoke in my face.

"I ain't no damn charity case." I laughed and grabbed my bag.

"You comin' or nah?" Jazelle put out her blunt and followed me out the door. Loyal did his best to keep me away from Jazzy, and she tried her best to stay close.

"YEAH, I remember. That was the day you and Loyal became enemies." We shared a laugh, and then Jazelle got serious.

"All bullshit aside, I love you, Kay. I'm glad you're okay."

"I know." I turned to walk out, and she grabbed my arm.

"How much time you think we got left?"

"Be cool, Jazelle." I pulled my arm away and walked out.

"Hey guys, y'all ready to go home?" Mama turned around like I had just asked everybody to toot some powder.

"Why would you go back there? It's plenty of room here." She spread out her arms.

"She'll be fine Mama Lena; I got her." Bryson walked over and wrapped his arms around my waist.

"No offense Bryson, but you had her last time." She put had in air quotes. Bryson raised his hands and backed away from me.

"Mama! We will be fine at home with Bryson." I looked over my shoulder at Jazelle. Kai stood up and ran up the hall.

"I'm going to get my stuff! Uncle B, you wanna play the game when we get home?" Bryson walked off behind her. I turned and looked back at mama.

"I got this, mama. I'm much better now that Loyal is gone. Everything will be fine. What else could go wrong?" I hugged her and Kenedee and made my way out to the car where Bryson and Kai were already waiting. Bryson was grinning from ear to ear. I couldn't help but feel happy. Things were finally starting to look up.

8

JAZELLE

I went back into Kadence's room and stared at the picture of the three of us. It seemed so long ago. It was crazy to me how much shit had gone down in the last ten years. Kadence and I remembered that day a little differently though.

I HAD JUST FINISHED WASHING the dishes to help Kadence with her chores so we could hit the streets. Mama Lena and Kenedee were gone, and we were trying to be gone already before they came back. There was a knock at the door, and I turned around to see Loyal standing in the screen door.

"Hey whassup?"

"Is Kadence around?"

"She ran to the store to get something for dinner. She should be back any minute now."

"Mind if I wait?" Loyal sat down at the table without waiting for an answer. As I put away the dishes, I could feel him staring at me.

"What are you looking at?" Loyal smiled.

"Nothing." He got up and walked over to me, pressing me up against the kitchen counter.

"What are you doing?"

"Nothing that you don't want me to."

Loyal reached around me and unbuttoned my pants. He licked his finger and slid it inside my shorts. I don't know what came over me, but suddenly I needed to feel him inside of me. My pussy was throbbing. Loyal put his hand on my shoulder, and I bent over the sink. I heard him tear the condom open and grunt as he slid inside me. Loyal felt so good; no wonder Kadence didn't have time for me like she used to. I gripped his dick with my pussy and moaned.

"You bet not ever tell my girl," Loyal grabbed my dreads and whispered in my ear.

"I won't," I moaned. "Just don't stop."

I threw it back as Loyal drilled me, causing my knees to bang against the cabinets. Loyal grabbed my hips and moaned as I came on his dick. I looked up and saw Kadence pulling in the driveway.

"Move!" I threw my ass back as hard as I could, and Loyal moaned so loud I was surprised Kadence didn't hear from the car. "Kadence is here; I said move!" Loyal took a step back and pulled his pants up. I fixed my shorts and started walking towards the bathroom to freshen up.

"Hey, babe! What are you doing here?" I turned around just in time to see them hugging each other.

"I came to see you. What you cookin'?" I closed the door on the rest of their conversation.

They were barely two weeks in, and he was already cheating. I mean I know I was just as wrong as he was, but it was normal for girls to send a decoy in to see how their man behaved. Kadence just wasn't aware yet. I planned to tell her to break up with Loyal without having her hate me as well. I freshened up and walked back to the kitchen.

"Hey Jazzy, Loyal wants to go to the movies, you down?" I rolled my eyes and shook my head.

"Naw, I thought we had plans, but I guess I'll just go home."

"Don't be like that. You can join us. You don't mind do you, babe?" Loyal shook his head. He was hesitant to look me in the eyes.

"Jazelle probably got her own date," he said as he concentrated on his phone.

"You know what? Actually I don't. I'm down to go." Kadence smiled.

"Great! This should be fun." She started dinner, and we went to the movies. The vibe was different between us now. Kadence sat between the two of us.

"Why are y'all actin so funny?" she whispered to me as the previews were playing. Before I could answer, Loyal pulled Kadence over towards him.

"Why she always got to follow us around?" Kadence shushed him and focused on the screen. It was sad how oblivious she was to the fact that Loyal wasn't shit.

I stuck the picture in my bag and went to say goodbye to Mama Lena. I could do without seeing Kenedee again, but they were literally all I had.

"Mama, I'm going to get out of here."

"You're leaving so soon?"

"Yeah, I got a few errands to run," I lied. Kenedee looked up at me.

"Come on, Jazelle. Let me walk you out." She stood to her feet and waited for me to walk out of the kitchen. Thinking about the person she was, I waited.

"You can go first." I held my hand out, and she walked up the hall. It was no secret that I had never been Kenedee's favorite person, but I admired her. All of a sudden, she had heart. This was not the prissy Ken that I had grown up with. She walked out on the porch and stared at me.

"What's going on, Jazzy?" For a second, I almost thought she cared.

"Nothing."

"You sure?" I nodded my head, and Kenedee took a step closer to me.

"I don't know where your head is, but I need you to understand, I will kill you about my sister. This ain't no motherfuckin' joke." Kenedee bumped me with her shoulder as she walked back inside the house. "Dumb bitch." She slammed the door behind her.

I laughed and walked to my car. I couldn't stop thinking about the exchange between Kadence and Ashlee. Honestly, I was more than a little shook. I drove up the street, and my mind would not stop racing.

I pulled into a bar and parked. Yes, it was still morning, but if they were open, I didn't see any harm in having one drink. I got out, and the owner was just opening up.

"Mind if I come in?" I walked up towards the door.

"Come on in, beautiful." He held the door open for me. I sat down at the bar. "What can I get you?" he asked.

"Double shot of Henny; make that two." He nodded his head and walked off. The bartender looked old enough to be my daddy. I looked around, and I could tell this bar held a whole lot of secrets.

"Wanna talk about it?" He asked as he slid the shot glasses in front of me.

"About what?"

"The fact that it's barely eleven o'clock and you've already had four shots." I laughed and slid the glasses back. I sat a $50 bill on the counter.

"Well, give me four more." He did as he was told. I downed the first shot as a man closer to my age walked in.

"Rough morning?" he asked as he sat beside me.

"Since when did everybody in the damn bar become so friendly?" He looked at me for a second, before moving to another empty barstool.

"Let me get a double shot of Henny and give the angry lady whatever she's having." The bartender laughed. He poured six shots and gave four to me. The younger man smiled.

"Straight Henny, no chaser, huh?" I rolled my eyes at him.

"What do you want?" For the first time since he walked in, I paid attention to him. He was fine! In a gray three-piece suit with Stacy Adams made me wonder what the hell he was doing in a bar so early.

"My name is Royce. I don't mean no harm, ma'am."

"Ma'am? I'm younger than you!" My words were slurring as I moved closer to him. He laughed showing off his dimples. The scent of his cologne filled my nostrils, and it immediately reminded me of Bryson.

"My bad, I was taught to call a lady ma'am if you haven't been properly introduced. Like I said, my name is Royce." He extended his hand and stared at me.

"I'm Jazelle." I shook his head and smiled. "What are you doing here, Royce?"

"The same as you." He smiled, and I couldn't help but smile back. "Wanna talk about it?" I shrugged my shoulders.

"My sister hates me. And I don't think she'll ever love me again." Royce's smile faded as he handed me his shot.

"What did you do, if you don't mind my asking?" I dropped my head. I was suddenly embarrassed about the shit I had done over the past few weeks. I started to question myself on if it was really worth it.

"A bunch of bullshit."

"That bad, huh?" I nodded my head and took another shot. The room was starting to spin. The bartender walked over to us.

"Can I get y'all anything else?" I started to order another shot, but Royce spoke for me.

"I don't think she needs it. I'm good also."

"Don't fuckin' speak for me, sitting over there in a business suit! Why yo ass ain't at work anyway." Royce smiled.

"Did you drive here?" I nodded my head.

"Yes, and I need to get home." I stood to my feet and lost my balance. Royce helped me up.

"I can drive you home. I wouldn't be a man if I let you drive like this."

"Mm-hmm. You just wanna see where I live." I stumbled to the car relying heavily on Royce to keep me off the ground. He helped me into the passenger seat of my car.

"Where do you live?" I told him my address and got comfortable.

"You know how people say blood is thicker than water? I don't believe that shit at all. The only blood I have in the world, switched up on me. And then there's you, the motherfuckin' water here to save the day!" Royce chucked as he drove in the lunch hour traffic.

"I'm happy I could be there for you."

We made small talk the rest of the drive. He pulled my car into the driveway and helped me out of the car. After making sure I was safely inside, he pulled out his phone.

"I'm gonna call an Uber to get back to my car."

"Or you could stay. You know and have lunch with me." Royce looked at his phone again and smiled.

"I'd like that. What's for lunch?" He followed me into the kitchen where I searched through the cabinets for something to cook.

"Why don't you let me cook for you?"

Royce helped me over to the table. He started a pot of coffee and pulled out ingredients for an omelet. I laid my head down on the table and waited for the nausea to go away. Royce hummed while he cooked. Somehow, it relaxed me a little. I looked up from the table just in time to see Royce snort a line from the counter. I put my head back on the table and tried to convince myself that my eyes were playing tricks on me. I looked up again as he snorted another. I got up from the table and walked over to him.

"How does it make you feel?" Royce jumped and turned to face me.

"I can show you better than I can tell you." He wiggled the small vile with the powdery substance inside.

"Okay," I whispered as Royce flipped the omelet. He dropped a line for me and handed me a small golden straw.

"Take your time. Do it slowly. It might burn a little but just keep going the high will be better than any blunt you ever had."

I twirled the straw in my hand and smiled I followed Royce's instructions. I felt like my head would burst open and then like I was floating in the air. I could hear Royce talking, but he sounded far away. I wrapped my arms around his neck and pulled him close to me. Royce leaned in and kissed me.

"You okay?" He pressed his forehead against mine.

"Yes. I like this."

I tried to focus on one thing but I couldn't. It was like every thought that I'd ever had was running through my mind right now. Royce lifted my chin and kissed me again. The smoke alarm started to ring, and Royce pushed the pan from the stove and lifted me on the counter. I wrapped my legs around him and pulled him close.

"You sure you wanna do this?" he whispered in my ear. I nodded my head and slid my panties to the side. Royce and I made love on my counter top twice that day. We never did eat the omelets; we just spent the day making one another feel better.

9

BRYSON

Kai and I were playing Mortal Kombat. Kadence was stretched out on the couch smiling at the both of us. It was almost as if the last few weeks had never happened. My phone started to vibrate, and I ignored it the first time, but it wouldn't stop. I answered the unknown call the usual way.

"Who the fuck is this?" Kai burst into giggles, and Kadence gave me that look all mothers get when you do something bad around their children. I shrugged my shoulders.

"Whassup bro, this is Braylon. There were some lil' niggas from up the way asking about them stick up girls too." I looked over at Kadence and paused the game.

"I'll be right back, baby girl," I told Kai and walked through the house and out the back door. I pressed the phone closer to my ear. "What they say?"

"They said they were looking for some bad ass bitches that got down on them. Said they took everything they had and went to the police."

"You get a pic?"

"A pic? Nigga what the fuck! Am I supposed to say pose for this selfie? Naw, I ain't get no fuckin' pic. The lil' nigga left his number though in case I heard something."

"Text it to me."

"Yeah, aight. Who are these bitches everybody on the lookout for?"

"Nobody you need to worry about. I'll hit your line in a minute. It's family time right now." Braylon laughed.

"King B out here playin' daddy. Who would have thought?" It was true; having kids had always been the furthest thing from my mind. Money was always the motive behind every move I made.

"Funny how shit changes, ain't it?" I laughed myself. I looked in the window and checked on my girls through the window. Kai had un-paused the game, and I'm almost positive that she was cheating and beating my ass while I wasn't looking.

"Hold on to that shit. You never know when you'll need your family."

"Yeah, yeah." I brushed him off already knowing where this conversation was going. "What was the nigga name?"

"The nigga said his name was Zee." I had heard of a nigga named Zee in Beloit, but I knew he worked for Raekwon, and Jazelle and Kadence couldn't be in deep enough to be robbing him.

"Aight bro. Hit my line later." I hung up the phone and walked back to the living room.

"Is everything okay, Bryson?" Kadence looked up at me.

Everything that I thought I knew about her was a lie, but she was carrying my seed, so I was fuckin' with her regardless. She was giving me something that no other broad I fucked with could, and I loved her more than anything for that alone.

"Yeah, everything's good. You hungry?"

I sat down and picked up the controller. Just as I suspected the game was over and Kai's character was jumping up and down claiming to be the winner, while mine was laid out bleeding all over the damn place. She smiled up at me and started a rematch.

"I don't need to eat every 20 minutes, man." She sat up on the couch and looked out the window.

"Don't be tryin' to starve my baby. You better eat."

I pretended to press the buttons. Kai was so into the game that she was standing up pressing every button on the controller at the same time. I sat it down on the floor and leaned over to rub Kadence's foot. She leaned back on the couch and closed her eyes. The doorbell rang, and Kai ran to it. She reached for the knob and then pulled her hand back.

"Mommy, should I open the door?"

"Naw, I got it." I ran to the door and waited until Kai was back focused on the game. I opened the door and stared at the girl standing on the porch.

"Hey, is Kenedee here?" She tried to look past me, but I blocked her view. I knew Kenedee wasn't one to hang with other females outside of her sisters, so this girl showing up was suspect.

"Who are you?" She rolled her eyes and flicked the ashes from her cigarette in Kadence's bushes.

"Is she here or not?" I started to close the door, but she stuck her foot in it.

"Okay, my name is Paris. She knows me." I eyed her up and down.

"Naw, Kenedee doesn't live here." I tried to push the door closed again, and she pushed it back open.

"Look, lady—" she cut me off.

"Tell Kenedee she needs to call me as soon as fuckin' possible." I laughed.

"I don't know who you think you're scaring or why you think I have to pass any messages for you." I pushed her off the porch and closed the door.

"Who the fuck is Paris?" I walked back to the living room and asked Kadence.

"I think that's the girl Kenedee used to go to school with. Why?"

"She was at the door." I left the rest out. I didn't know how Kadence would react and I ain't want no more bodies on her hands. "You know somebody named Zee?" She shook her head quickly.

"Naw, it doesn't sound familiar. Who is that?"

"Nobody." She frowned her face.

"You're asking a lot of questions to keep saying never mind." I sat on the couch next to her and started rubbing her feet again.

"I'm just tryin' to see what you remember," I played it off. Kadence rolled her eyes and focused on the TV. "I gotta make a run right quick. Want me to pick something up for lunch?" Kadence nodded her head.

"You or Kai can choose. I'm gonna go take a shower. Kai, will you be okay down here alone?"

"I'm a big girl, mommy. You don't have to stay in the same room with me."

"Okay, I'll be upstairs if you need me." She headed to the door. "Don't open the door for anyone. Bryson has a key." Kai nodded her head without looking up from her game.

As soon as Kadence was upstairs, I pulled out my phone and dialed the number. Zee answered on the first ring.

"Yo?"

"Yeah, I heard you were lookin' for somebody."

"Who the fuck is this?" I cleared my throat already annoyed with him.

"Nigga, you came to my hood asking questions. Show some fuckin' respect." Zee softened his tone.

"Who this?"

"King B. You heard of me?" Zee was quiet for a few minutes.

"Yeah, I heard of you. Whassup?" I smiled and started my car. It was nice to know my name still rang in these streets.

"What you lookin' for them girls for?"

"They got down on me. Took all my shit, and I need that back ASAP."

"How much they get you for?"

"Shit, the whole motherfuckin' shipment." I leaned against the banister and looked in the house. "I need all that shit back." Zee continued. "You know where I can find them?"

"I might know where they are. You still in Madison?"

I walked over to the garage and pulled my toolbox from under a table where Kadence kept the sewing machine she never used. I opened it and made sure my pistols were still there. I had to keep them close by, but I didn't want Kadence to know where they were.

"I can be. This shit is important."

"Aight man, hit my line when you make it." I went back in the house and busted in on Kadence's shower.

"Yo, get out the shower. We need to talk." She stuck her head out and smiled at me.

"Or you can come join me." As bad as I wanted to join her, I needed some answers first.

"You know a nigga named Zee?" Kadence stuck her head out of the shower again.

"Why do you ask?" I leaned against the sink and stared at her.

"You know why I'm asking." She went back in the shower, and a few seconds later the water turned off. Kadence stepped out the shower, and my dick instantly got hard.

"What about him?" She wrapped herself in a towel and moved closer to me.

"Is he looking for you?" Kadence laughed and went to get dressed. I could hear the nervousness in her laugh.

"No. Why would he be looking for me?" She opened and closed all of her drawers without pulling anything out.

"He came to the hood looking for two pretty girls that took his whole shipment. That wasn't y'all was it?"

"That was not a whole fuckin' shipment, and if it was he needs to be ashamed of himself!" she snapped and then looked up at me with her big gray eyes.

"Damn, Kadence." She rushed over to me with fear in her eyes.

"I'm sorry. I should have known his persistent ass would find us after what happened."

"When were you gonna tell me what happened?" I sat down on the bed. "I thought we agreed no more secrets. She looked at me for a few seconds and then ran down the story of her run-in with Zee. I stared at her wondering how she and Jazelle had so much going on behind my back.

"So where's the money?" Kadence frowned at me.

"It's put up for my children. Why?" I laughed.

"Calm down, beautiful. Don't nobody want your money. I just need to know what I'm walking into."

"What do you mean?"

"Baby, I told you I got you. As long as you're the mother of my child, you never have to worry about anything." She sat down on my lap and wrapped her legs around me. "At the same time, you have to let me know everything. I can't be hearing shit about you from niggas on the street." Kadence nodded her head and kissed me.

"Yes, daddy. Do you need me to do anything?" I shook my head and lifted her in the air.

"Just have my dinner ready when I get back." She smiled and kissed me again.

"I love you, Bryson."

"Not as much as I love you." I sat her down and sent a text to Braylon.

Me: Get ready. Omw to pick you up.

Braylon: Yup.

I checked on Kai before leaving to meet up with this nigga.

"You need anything, baby girl?" She shook her head and waved over her shoulder.

"Nope. Be careful. I want you to come back." No matter how tough I was, I would always have a soft spot for them.

10

KENEDEE

I woke up to a text that I knew would be coming sooner rather than later.

Daddy: I need to see you Kenedee. Plz call.

I sat the phone down and got out the bed to check on mama. She had been sleeping in that damn chair all night and complained about the pain all morning. She was still snoring, so I walked back to the room to get my stuff and stepped out on the porch to smoke before she woke up. As soon as my ass hit the chair, my phone started to ring.

"Hello?" I usually didn't answer unknown calls, but I had the feeling they wouldn't stop until I did.

"Kenedee, how are you?" I looked up and saw the black Chevy Impala parked across the street.

"Whitney? What are you calling me for?" I recognized her voice immediately. I pulled the blade that I had tucked in mama's flowerpot next to the chair.

"Why won't you leave Kyle alone?" Her voice was low. Just the sound of it put me on edge.

"A better question would be, why won't Kyle leave me alone?" I hit the blunt, letting the smoke fill my lungs. I kept my eyes on the car just in case it was this psychotic bitch.

"He hasn't called you. I keep seeing messages from you in his phone, and I cannot figure out for the life of me why you will not just find your own man." I laughed loudly into the phone.

"No, ma'am. Your husband is cheating on you with someone else. Ain't no way in hell he could even smell this pussy again."

I hung up and blocked my phone from accepting unknown calls. If she wanted to talk to me again, she would have to pull up or call straight through. The fact that she knew everything about me and I was totally clueless about her bothered the hell out of me. I stood and walked to the edge of the porch and looked out into the street. It was early, so the streets were packed with people leaving for work.

Daddy: I need to speak with you. Where are you?

My phone buzzed in my hand, and I nearly dropped it. I quickly blocked his number as well. Stalking was at an all-time with them people, and I could not deal. I sent a text to Kadence. That girl woke up at the crack of dawn and I knew she would be awake.

Me: Morning Kay. Give Kai kisses and tell her to have a good day for me. She replied instantly. It amazed me how that girl texted so fast.

Kadence: Morning Ken. I will and why don't you come over for lunch tomorrow. We haven't had a sister day in a while. I told her I would be there and went back inside the house.

I slid the chain across the door and went back to my room. Mama was still snoring, and as long as she was getting some sleep, I would let her. I crawled back under the covers and pulled out my Kindle. Latoya Nicole had just dropped the finale to *Love and War: A Hoover Gang Affair,* and I needed my daily dose of Blaze. That nigga was funny as fuck! I heard someone knocking at the door, and I knew it was only a matter of time before mama was awake and telling me to get up and do something, so I beat her to the door. I swung the door open and stood face to face with Kyle.

"What the hell are you doing at my mother's house, Kyle?" He peeked around behind me.

"I said we need to talk." I pushed open the screen and stepped on the porch. The Impala that was parked across the street was now gone.

"Talk about what? You can't just pull up on me whenever you feel like it. We not rockin' like that no more."

Kyle stood there staring at me with a smile on his face. I would be lying if I said he wasn't looking fine as hell standing there looking all pitiful. For a second, I almost wanted to wrap my arms around him and let him take all my troubles away. But then, I remembered all the hell I had gone through because of him.

"I miss you, baby girl."

"You shouldn't. Where is your wife? You know she probably got a lo jack on you." We both started laughing. Kyle took a step closer to me and put his hand against the house. He moved his body to the other side so that I was blocked in.

"I can't let you leave me, Kens."

"You can't stop me, Kyle." I tried to push past him, but he was way stronger than he appeared.

"I'm done playing these games with you. I paid more than enough for the ten fuckin' minutes of your time that I am asking for." Kyle had a tight grip on my arm. "Now, let's go talk."

He pulled me towards the edge of the porch, and I reached down in the flowerpot. Before we made it to the stairs, I flipped open the blade and slid it across the outside of Kyle's wrist. He screamed out and jumped away from me.

"I told you, we ain't got shit to talk about!" I ran into the house locking the door behind me.

"Kenedee? What's all that noise out there?" I slid the blade into my shorts and headed to the bathroom.

"Nothing, mama. Let's go out for breakfast today!" I yelled as I rinsed his blood from the blade. My phone started to vibrate. I looked at the screen, and it was Kadence.

"I'm so glad you called. I need your help." I agreed to meet Kadence after breakfast with mama. When I came out of the bathroom, I could smell that mama was making a pot of coffee.

"Ma, I said we were going out for breakfast." I walked into the kitchen and saw Kyle sitting at the table with a mug in his head.

"Oh, there she is. Ken, your professor wanted to stop by and speak with you about your grade." My heart felt like it could leap out of my chest any second.

"They send emails for that." Mama grabbed my arm and pushed me down in the chair.

"Where are your manners?" She poured coffee into Kyle's cup. "So how is Kenedee doing, professor?" Kyle took a sip of his coffee and smiled at me.

"Well, actually Ms. Jones, I'm here because I'm concerned about Kenedee's grade. She hasn't been to class much at all this semester. I know how important my class is to her major." My blood was boiling. I looked down at his wrist, and the sleeve of his suit was stained with blood.

"Professor Hughes, can I speak you outside?"

"Of course." He stood up and sat his mug on the table. As soon as I closed the door behind us, I smacked him upside his head.

"What the fuck is that?" I folded my arms across my chest and stared at him.

"You know how sexy you look when you're mad?" He took a step closer to me. "Your mom was ready to invite me to dinner, huh? Maybe I'll come back and talk to her since you don't want to talk to me." I rolled my eyes.

"Kyle—" He cut me off and put a hotel room key in my hand.

"Meet me at seven, or I'll be back at eight." Kyle turned and walked towards his car with a smile on his face. I stood in the porch, not really sure what to do. When I came back in, mama was dressed and sitting in her favorite chair.

"He seemed like a nice man." I nodded my head and went to grab my bag. I checked my phone and had two unread messages. One was from Kyle and the other from an unknown number.

"Don't say I didn't try to warn you, bitch." I slid my phone back down in my purse and walked back to the living room.

"Where you wanna go eat, mama? My treat." She smiled and stood to her feet.

"I get to choose, and you're paying? Why did you do?" She laughed and kissed me on the cheek as I held the door open for her. I looked up and down the street. There was no suspicious cars or people, so I walked out and turned to lock the door behind me.

I HEARD an unfamiliar voice ask mama, "Excuse me, ma'am. Can you tell me where the bus stop is?" Mama always being her helpful self stepped off the porch.

"Well, there's no bus that comes here, baby. Where you headed?" I turned around to see the young man; he couldn't have been any older than me. He pulled two pistols from his pants and aimed one at each of us.

"Go back in the house!" he growled in a voice that was completely different from the voice that he had used before.

"Oh no, baby what are you doin'?" mama asked him, and he pushed the gun in her side.

"Unlock the door now!" I fumbled with the keys trying to figure out what the hell was going on here.

"Who sent you here?" I asked, putting the key in the door and opening it. He pushed us inside. I looked around for anything to defend my mama and me. There was nothing that could go up against a gun.

"Call your sister." Confused, I turned around to face him.

"My sister?"

"Did I fuckin' stutter? Call the bitch right now!" he yelled in my face. I pulled my phone from my bag. I made sure I turned the volume all the way down. I had no idea who he was talking about so I called the only person I thought could help me at the moment. Bryson answered on the first ring.

"Whassup Kenedee?"

"I need you to get here now. Somebody is looking for you, Kay."

"Somebody like who?" Bryson asked.

"I don't know. He won't tell me who he is. He's really pissed and wants you here now."

"Fuck! I'm on my way. Gimme two minutes." I hung up the phone and looked at him.

"She's on her way." I stared at the man. Madison was a big ass town, but I was sure he wasn't from here. There was something different about him.

"How do you know Kadence?" mama asked him. He had taken the gun away from her but kept them pointed at me.

"No talkin! Just sit down and wait for her to show." We did as we were told.

A few seconds later, I heard the music from Bryson's truck as he pulled up. I squeezed mama's hand and waited. She looked back and forth between the man and me. Her face was full of worry. I heard the keys in the door. I took a deep breath and prepared myself for whatever hell that was gonna let loose when Bryson walked through that door.

"Whassup?" Bryson walked in with a man I had never seen before. The man raised his gun at me and cocked the trigger.

"Who the fuck is this? I said call your fuckin' sister!" Bryson stepped in between the gun and I. His friend, who looked a lot like him grabbed mama's hand.

"Ms. Jones, let's get you out of here." He smiled at me and helped mama out the back door.

"My man, chill. Kadence is my wife. What's the problem?" Bryson was cool as hell to have a pistol pointed in his face. I wanted to run for safety, but a part of me needed to know what happened next.

"Your wife owes me ten bands, and I need all that." Bryson laughed.

"My wife owes you ten bands? Really?" Bryson dropped his ass with a right hook before the man could answer. The man flew into the glass coffee table. "What the fuck are you doing here lil' nigga?" Bryson stomped the man in his face. "Your mama ain't teach you to respect ya fuckin' elders? Huh, motherfucka!" Bryson screamed in his now bloodied face. I had never seen this side of Bryson, but I now knew exactly what had my sisters losing their damn minds. The other guy came back in and smiled at me. He stretched out his hand.

"I'm Braylon, Bryson's big brother," he casually said like Bryson wasn't beat a man half to death less than five feet away.

"Um, Kenedee. Where's my mother?" He pointed to the window.

"She's outside in the car. You two go on to breakfast. We got this."

I was reluctant to leave, but I did as I was told. I walked through the house towards the back where mama had gone. I could hear the man crying to Bryson that he was sorry and Bryson telling him that it was too late to be sorry. I pulled out my phone and called Kadence.

"Hey Ken," she answered cheerfully.

"Okay, I need to know what the fuck you have going on." I could tell Kadence was hesitant.

"What do you mean?"

"What do you really know about Bryson?" I sat down in the car and sped out of there as fast as I could. Kadence was going to have to explain this shit whether she wanted to or not.

11

KADENCE

I had no idea what the hell Kenedee was talking about, but I suspected she would be on my doorstep at any moment. I walked downstairs and sat down next to Kai. I grabbed the jewelry box that was on the coffee table and turned the TV off.

"Kai, I got something for you." She turned and stared at me.

"What is it, mommy?" I opened the box and pulled the 24K gold chain with a small gold key charm attached to it.

"This goes to the safety deposit box down at mommy's bank. You remember which one?" Kai nodded her head and turned around so that I could put the chain on her.

"Never take this off. If anything happens to mommy, you give that key to granny or Auntie Ken only. Nobody else okay." Kai nodded her head again. A smile started to come on her face.

"Is this our little secret, mommy?"

"Sure is. Nobody knows about this box but you and me. So let's keep it that way." Kai nodded her head and stared the out the window.

"Mommy?" I pulled her close to me.

"Yes, baby?"

"Nothing else is gonna happen to you, right?" I squeezed her tight.

"As long as I can help it, baby. I'll be around as long as I can."

I kissed the top of her forehead. Satisfied with my answer, Kai cuddled next to me on the couch. We watched whatever show she was watching before I came in. At that moment, I felt like life was good. I wasn't worried about anything, but what my family was going to have for dinner. I rubbed my belly and closed my eyes. My phone rang, and Bryson's picture filled the screen.

"Hey babe, whassup?" He was out of breath, and I could hear the attitude in his voice.

"Get a room ready for your mom and sister. They're staying with us for a few days."

"My mom? Why would they be coming here?"

"I'll explain when I get there. I told them to come over and stay there until I get back. And find a way to get Jazelle dumb ass over there too." I sat up and looked out the window. For some reason, I felt time we were in danger.

"Babe, you're scaring me."

"Scared for what. Ya man got you. I just need to keep an eye on y'all. I'll be home soon. But get them ready now." Bryson hung up before I could say anything else. I called Kenedee, and she answered quickly.

"We're about to pull up now. Bitch, we need answers." I could hear my mother fussing at Kenedee to watch her mouth. I got up and waited for them on the porch. A few minutes later, Kenedee came around the corner practically on two wheels. Mama jumped out the car and ran to me.

"Are you okay?" She pulled me into a hug and kissed both my cheeks.

"I'm fine, mama. Are you okay?" She nodded her head and walked inside.

"That Braylon is a good man. I wouldn't be if it weren't for him." Kenedee walked up behind mama with a blunt hanging from her mouth.

"Who's Braylon, and what are you doing smoking? What the hell did I miss?" I sat down on the porch swing, and Kenedee sat beside me.

"Braylon is Bryson's older brother. Bryson is a real life goon." I laughed.

"Bryson is not a goon."

"Some nigga came to the house looking for you. He said you owed him ten bands. Bryson stomped his ass out and told us to come here and wait." I studied Ken's face to see if she was joking or not. She inhaled the smoke and blew it away from me.

"Bryson stomped a nigga out?" My thoughts immediately turned to Zee. Did that nigga really have enough heart to pull up to my mom's house? I called Bryson, but his phone was going straight to voicemail. I called Jazelle.

"Hello?" She sounded like she was still asleep.

"Wake up. I need you to come over." She exhaled deeply.

"Kadence, I can't. I'll call you later." She hung up on me.

"Who was that?" Kenedee asked. She was now pacing the floor, looking at everything around her. I tried to call Jazelle again, and now her phone went straight to voicemail too.

"You need to stop smoking that shit. You look crazy." Kenedee rolled her eyes at me.

"It's been people comin' for me all day. I need to be aware of my surroundings."

"Who's coming for you?" I asked, standing to my feet. "What's going on?"

"The nigga with the gun looking for you first off, and Kyle showed up this morning too."

"Kyle? The professor?" I rolled my eyes. Kenedee and that man's drama was going to kill me before any of these bitch ass niggas could.

"It's not what you think. He's stalking me, Kay. I'm trying to leave him alone." Kenedee looked like she was on the verge of a breakdown. I decided I wouldn't even tell her about Paris showing up, but I did plan to get to the bottom of it.

"Why didn't you tell me?" I wrapped my arms around her and

pulled her into the house. Mama and Kai were watching TV. We walked down to the guest room and sat on the daybed. Kenedee wiped her eyes and stared at me.

"He even got mama thinking he's a good dude."

"What did he say to mama?"

"He fuckin' told her I was flunkin' out! That he came by because he was worried about my grade." I couldn't contain my laughter.

"Mama ain't no dummy, Ken. She let it go for now, but know that she gone ask about it later." Kenedee nodded her head and wiped her tears.

"I know. I just didn't know what to say then. Breakfast was supposed to be a distraction, but then dude showed up." The wheels in my head were turning full speed.

"He specifically asked for me by name?"

"No, he kept saying call your sister. But when Bryson showed up he said your wife." I stood up and walked towards the door.

"Nobody knows I'm with Bryson though." I went to my room, grabbed my Beretta, and stuck it in my purse. Kenedee was on my heels.

"Where are you going though?"

"To find Bryson." I stepped out on the porch and Bryson was pulling in behind Kenedee's car. He got out and smiled, followed by another nigga that looked like a slightly older version of him.

"Where do you think you're going?" Bryson kissed me and took my purse from me. "You don't need that." He laughed and turned to his brother.

"Braylon, this is Kadence. Kadence, this is my big brother." Braylon pulled me into a bear hug with a huge smile on his face.

"Nice to meet you, sis." He rubbed my belly. "How's my nephew doing in there?"

"Fine. Nice to meet you too, Braylon. How come we never heard about you?" Braylon shrugged his shoulders and looked at Bryson.

"My brother doesn't like to talk about where he comes from." Bryson wrapped his arms around my waist, sliding my purse back on my arm.

"You don't need to know about that nigga. I was a different person back then." Kenedee stood and stared up at Braylon who towered over her.

"I wanna know about the old him. Because I need some answers about what the hell I just saw." Braylon held out his arm, and Kenedee linked hers inside.

"How about we get better aquatinted then?" Kenedee smiled and led him inside the house. I turned and wrapped my arms around Bryson's neck.

"Did Zee go to my mom's house?" Bryson shook his head.

"Ken said the guy was looking for me."

"You heard from Jazelle?" That was the second time that day he had asked me about her.

"Why?"

"Because that's who robbed him. That's who he was after. I never made it to meet with Zee because Kenedee called going crazy bout needing you to pull up. I couldn't let that happen, so I went in your place." The love I had for Bryson was growing stronger and stronger by the day. The way that he held me and my family down with no questions asked amazed me.

"So what did you do to him?" I asked a small part of me was excited.

"Nothin' major." Bryson shrugged his shoulders.

"Come on! Ken said you were a real life goon." Bryson laughed and shook his dreads. I looked him up and down and noticed the blood splatter on his shoes and the bottom of his jeans.

"I'm just regular old B. Ain't shit special about me."

"Really?" He nodded his head.

"Yeah, really." He followed my gaze to the blood. "That ain't nothing." Bryson grabbed my hand and pulled me into the house.

I watched as Braylon told stories of him and Bryson growing up in the hood. We walked into the bedroom, and I told him about Kenedee's situation. Bryson shook his head. My mama was right when she said the pretty girls get you in trouble."

"Please don't ever think I can't hold my own." Bryson gripped my chin and kissed me gently.

"You fuckin' with a real nigga now, so you ain't gotta hold shit." I nodded my head while planning a way to take matters into my own hands. As if he could read my mind, Bryson stared into my eyes.

"I mean it, Kadence. Keep my fuckin' baby safe. All this bullshit is none of your concern. I got this. You take care of this." He put his hand over my stomach. I nodded my head.

"Okay, baby."

"I'm going to find Jazelle. I need to know what the fuck she's been out here doing."

"You're going to her house?" I asked, getting up from the bed.

"Yeah. Whassup?" I didn't feel right telling him that I didn't want him alone with her, so I just shook my head.

"Be careful, and tell her to call me." Bryson nodded his head. He leaned in and kissed me.

"No stress, okay." Bryson kissed the tip of my nose. "Go enjoy your family. I'll be back soon." Bryson walked out of the room closing the door behind him.

I walked over to the window and watched him and Braylon get in his truck and pull off. I opened the safe that Loyal had installed in the back of my closet. I pulled the two .9mm with silencers from the safe. I pulled my bag from the floor and stuffed everything inside. I called Kenedee to come to my room while I searched through my drawers for something sexy to wear. She walked in and plopped down on the recliner.

"I have a plan. But first, I need to know how bad do you really want Kyle out of your life?"

Kenedee's leaned forward in her seat and smiled. "What kind of plan?"

12

JAZELLE

When I was finally able to get out of the bed, I called Kadence back. She didn't answer. I knew she was pissed that I had hung up on her. I rolled over and Royce was gone. I unplugged my phone and walked down to the kitchen. I started a lot of coffee and sat at the table scrolling they my Facebook feed. There was a knock at the door, and I was hesitant to answer because the last time I did, I got hauled off for questioning. I opened the door, and Bryson was standing there looking sexy as ever.

"Hey Bryson, what are you doing here?" He stepped in without waiting for an invitation. A part of me wanted to jump his bones right then and there, but I knew that chapter was closed.

"We need to talk." Bryson looked around the house and shook his head.

"You forgot how to clean up?" Feeling embarrassed, I started throwing things into a garbage bag.

"I haven't been home much. What's going on?" Bryson sat down on the couch and stared at me.

"What kind of shit you got going on?"

"Nothing." I knew exactly what he was talking about, but I wanted to see how much he knew first. Bryson exhaled deeply and stood up. He grabbed me by the chin and stared into my eyes.

"How long you been getting high, Jazelle?" I snatched away from him and continued to throw stuff in the garbage bag I was dragging behind me.

"I ain't getting high, Bryson. What's the problem?"

"A lil' nigga ran up in Mama Lena's house today. He said you got down on him and owed him ten bands. Now I'm out here cleaning up messes you left behind. So again I'mma ask you. What the fuck you got goin' on around here?" Bryson raised his voice, and it sent chills down my spine.

"I needed the money."

"If he can pull up to your mama house, that's too close to home. Jazzy, what's wrong with you?" It took everything in me not to break down and cry when he said my name. It had been so long since he even acknowledged my presence.

"We're here for you if you let us know what's going on." I turned to face Bryson, and the front door swung open. Royce walked in dressed in the same business suit he had been wearing when we first met.

"Hello?" he said, staring directly at Bryson. "What's he doing here?" I ran over to him, and he grabbed my arm and pulled me closer.

"He just came by to check on me." Royce dug his nails into my arm. I wanted to cry out, but I knew it would only make things worse. "But he was just leaving, right Bryson?" Bryson just stood there and stared at both of us.

"Tell mama I'll be there later. I just need to get dressed." Bryson still said nothing. Tears slowly slid down my face, and Bryson moved towards the door.

"Yeah, aight. Make sure you come to the house tonight, or I will be back." He looked at Royce once more, who still had not loosened his grip. Bryson pulled the door closed, and Royce finally let me go.

"You walking around naked in front of other niggas now?" Royce tugged at the boy shorts I was wearing.

"I was on my way to the bathroom when he came to the door." Royce grabbed a picture of Kadence and me from the coffee table and threw it across the room.

"You wear clothes whenever anybody steps foot in this house! If I wanted everybody to see what the fuck I had at home, I would have dated a fuckin' stripper!" Royce screamed, and the veins in his forehead looked like they would burst at any moment.

I examined my arm that still held the print of his nails. He sat down on the couch and sprinkled two lines of coke onto the table. He sniffed both and then passed the straw to me. As bad as I wanted it, I was scared to get close to him. Over a matter of days, Royce has changed into a completely different person. A part of me was afraid to leave him, and the other part loved having him around. I snorted my first line and leaned back on the couch. My phone was ringing loudly. I reached for it, and when I did, Kadence started screaming in my ear.

"Get over here now!"

"Okay. I'll over in a minute." I hung up the phone and looked at Royce who was already asleep.

I got dressed, grabbed my purse and keys, and headed to Kadence's house. I was desperate to spend some time with her. I missed the normal times that we shared. When I pulled up, she was wobbling back from the mailbox. She waved at me and slowly made her way to the house. I waited on the porch while she stopped to read an envelope.

"What's for lunch?" I asked taking a tissue from my purse and wiping my nose.

"Chicken lasagna." Kadence smiled and opened the door. My phone vibrated with a text from Royce.

Royce: Where are you?

Me: I had to go to my sister's house. I'll be back soon. I slid my phone in my pocket and followed Kadence. Royce had become super overprotective really fast.

Royce: How long is soon? Why didn't you tell me you were going somewhere?

I ignored his message and sat down at the table while Kadence set the table. I looked up and noticed that there were three plates.

"Who else is coming?" Before she could answer, Kenedee walked in the door. No matter what she was doing, Kenedee always looked like a movie star. She removed her oversized glasses and rolled her eyes at me.

"I thought you said sister lunch." Kadence sat the pan of lasagna on the table.

"I did. And now that all of us are here let's eat." Kenedee hesitated in the doorway, and Kadence sat a plate at her empty spot. "Sit down, Kenedee." She took her time sitting in the chair beside me. I was half expecting Kenedee to punch me or something.

Royce: Hello??

Kadence cleared her throat.

"This little beef that y'all have has gone on long enough. It's time to start acting like a family again." I looked back and forth between the two of them.

"Kenedee, I know I'm the last person that you want to build a relationship with. But she's right. You're my baby sister, and I love you." Kenedee stared at me for a few seconds. "I promise I'm not trying to steal Kadence away from you. I just want to be included." Kadence was stuffing her mouth with a huge grin on her face.

"See Ken, give her a chance." Kenedee rolled her eyes and picked up her fork.

"Jazelle, just don't do Kadence dirty. She rides for you unconditionally. If she can forgive you, so can I. Just know that you don't get as many chances from me as you do her.

Royce: You can't respond now.

Kenedee glanced over at my phone.

"Now, what was that shit that happened at mama's this morning?" Kadence asked. Her eyes were wild, and I knew she was struggling to keep her composure.

"It's already been handled." I waved it off. Kadence looked like she wanted to say more, but Kenedee cut her off.

"Is there a new man in your life, Jazzy?" I shrugged my shoulders while taking a bite of the food.

"I guess you could call him that." Royce and I weren't in a relationship at all. We got high and had amazing sex together. It was annoying when he blew up my phone knowing he didn't want a damn thing.

"You didn't tell me about a new boo thang," Kadence said, wiping her mouth and staring at me with a smile. Nobody outside of Royce knew about my new habit, and I planned to keep it that way. I didn't plan on getting high too much longer anyway. It was starting to take a toll on my savings account.

Royce: Okay, I ain't waiting for your ass then! Have fun with your fuckin' sister.

Just knowing that he was not going to wait made my stomach turn. I hurried and stuffed my food in my mouth. Both Kadence and Kenedee stared at me like I was crazy.

"You want some more, Jazzy?" I shook my head and jumped into the real reason I had agreed to lunch with Kadence.

"I actually wanted to talk to you about something."

"Okay, whassup?" Kenedee had stopped eating and was looking at me again.

"Have you thought about a job?" Kadence dropped her fork and cleared her throat.

"A job, Jazelle?" She motioned to the little pudge that was sticking from underneath the table.

"It wouldn't be much. I just need something." She looked over at Kenedee and back at me. Right on cue, Kenedee jumped in the conversation.

"What kind of job? I could use some money." Kadence stood up and walked over to the counter.

"This is not the kind of job for you," I spoke up.

"How you gone say what's right for her?" If looks could kill, I would have dropped dead on the spot.

"Shut the fuck up, Jazelle!"

"She's right though. I am old enough to speak for myself." She turned to me. "What kind of job is it? I mean you did say we needed to be more sister like and what not." I could see the anger growing inside of Kadence.

"So, what we do is—" Before I could say anything, Kadence cut me off.

"I said she's not ready. I got a mark planned out already." I smiled. I knew that Kadence would change her mind if Kenedee would get involved.

"I am not a fuckin' child. Now, what is the damn job?" Kadence rolled her eyes and plopped back down in her chair.

"We're stick up girls. We pick out niggas with hella money, get them all hot and bothered and then rob them. You think you could handle that?" I said quickly, with Kadence's eyes throwing daggers at me the entire time. Kenedee looked back and forth between the two of us.

"If anybody doesn't need to be doing it, it would be you." Kenedee reached out and rubbed Kadence's belly. "Put me on sis, Jazelle won't let nothing happen to me right?"

They both focused in on me. I pulled my phone from my purse and used my tissue to wipe my nose. Kenedee frowned her face up at me. "Are you sick, Jazelle?" Royce was calling now.

"No, I won't let you get sick," I mumbled and stood from the table. "I have to take this call."

"You tellin' me you wanna go rob niggas with her acting like that?" Kadence said as I walked into the living room. I dialed Royce's number, but he sent me to voicemail.

Me: Answer the phone. Wait for me!

I noticed Kadence's purse sitting on the arm of the couch. I looked in the kitchen to make sure they weren't checkin' for me. I walked over, pulled her wallet, pulled two one-hundred dollar bills out, and stuck them in my pocket. I had always told Kadence she carried too much money around on her and clearly, she still didn't believe me. I called Royce again, with no luck and headed back towards the kitchen.

"So, what's the verdict?"

"I'm going!" Kenedee pumped her fists in the air and laughed loudly. "What do I need to know?" Kenedee stared at me, and for a second, I wondered if I had made a mistake by even mentioning it to her. I cleared my throat and checked my phone again.

"Just be ready tomorrow. I'll call you in the morning to tell you what to pack." Kenedee nodded her head. "Thanks for lunch, Kay. I'll gotta get home though." Kadence nodded her head and started to clear the table

"I just got one question before you go. Weren't you the one who was scared to pull another job just a few months ago?" Both of them stared at me, waiting for an answer.

"A lot of shit has changed since then, hasn't it? Everybody ain't eatin' as good as you. I'll call you in the morning, Ken."

I hurried out the door. I knew that if Royce had stopped trying to get in touch with me, then he was probably already too far gone. I hurried to the apartment that we now shared. I opened the door and tripped over the pile of empty beer bottles that were scattered all over the living room.

"Royce?" I called as I walked into the bedroom. Royce was stretched out on the bed with the straw hanging from his fingertips. I reached for the straw and went to the vanity where I left my coke. Of course, it was gone. I kicked Royce until he was awake.

"Where is your car, Royce? You need to make a run." He rolled over and grunted.

"I sold it." I kicked him again because I knew I hadn't heard him correctly.

"You did what? Get the hell up!" Royce sat up in the bed and struggled to focus on me.

"Where is your car?"

"I already told you, I sold it." He rubbed his eye with one hand and wiped his runny nose with the other.

Royce got up and stumbled to the bathroom. I kicked the piles of dirty clothes out of the way and walked over to my dresser. I threw clothes out until I found my lucky shorts. I pulled purple bralette from the drawer and stuffed them both in my purse.

"What you packin' clothes for?" Royce stood behind me, blocking my path.

"I have to go out of town with my sister." Royce grabbed me by my neck, lifting me from the floor.

"I thought you said your sisters didn't fuck with you. Now all of a sudden, you got to do so much with them bitches!" Royce hissed at me as I struggled to breathe.

"Let go." I scratched at his arms, but it only made him squeeze tighter.

"Are you fuckin' around on me?" My head was pounding and everything was starting to go dark.

"Royce, please," I gasped. Royce smiled and dropped me to the floor hard.

"Stop fuckin' tryin' me, Jazelle." He pulled me from the floor by my hair. "You belong to me now." He walked back to the bathroom and slammed the door. I wiped my nose with my hand and went down to the kitchen. I poured a shot of Henny and sat at the bar.

What the fuck did I get myself into? I rolled my eyes and poured another shot. I heard a door slam, and then the doorbell rang. I looked out the window and saw Kadence standing outside my door tapping her foot.

"Open the damn door, Jazelle. I can fucking see you." I wiped my face and opened the door.

"Kadence, can we talk about this later."

"Hell no! We're talkin' now. You're doing way too much sneak shit, Jazelle. What the fuck was that about?" She pushed me out of the way and walked inside the house. Kadence looked around and frowned her face. "What's going on in here?"

"Nothing is going on." I blocked her from coming any further.

"Jazelle, seriously. What is going on with you?"

"Don't come in here acting like you give a fuck about me now. You ain't been caring about nobody but yourself. Oh and Kai." I wiped my nose, and Kadence started to look around the apartment again.

"Are you on that shit, Jazzy?"

"Get the fuck out, Kadence!" I was screaming at her. "How dare you come in my motherfuckin' house and insult me like that! Fuck you!" She was unbothered by my performance and had no problem showing it.

"Cut the dramatics. Why are you trying to bring Kenedee in after what happened last time? Like you ain't have motherfuckas holdin' mama at gunpoint this fuckin' morning! I thought you were good on pullin' licks."

"Like I said before, a lot of shit has changed since then."

"Why does your house look like this? Tell me what is going on."

"Kadence, you need to leave." Royce came down the stairs wearing nothing but a towel.

"Who is she?" Kadence stepped past me and stuck her head out to Royce.

"I'm her sister, who are you?"

"Her husband." Kadence looked at Royce and then over at me.

"You got married, Jazzy." I rolled my eyes and pulled her back towards the door by her arm.

"I will talk to you about it in the morning. I'll be over early." I loudly said because I knew Royce was listening. Kadence looked like she wanted to say more, but she didn't.

"I'll be here to pick you up at 6 a.m.," she said sternly, and I knew she meant it. As soon as Kadence was out the door, I turned around and ran right into Royce's fist.

"What did I do?" I covered my nose to stop the blood that was pouring out. Royce grabbed my hand and pulled me close to him.

"No more secrets, okay baby." He kissed my forehead and walked away.

Crying like a baby, I locked myself in the bathroom and tried to stop my nose from bleeding. It hurt so badly that I knew that it was broken. I waited until I heard the front door slam shut and my car pulling away. I went to the bedroom to get my purse and everything had been dumped onto the floor. My keys and the money I had taken from Kadence were missing. I took a shower and got in the bed. There was nothing I could do but wait for him to come home.

13

KENEDEE

Kadence had given me play-by-play instructions.

"You're sure you're done with him?" I nodded my head. Ashlee, Kadence's newfound friend did my makeup.

"Don't be nervous. If you're nervous, he will know something is up." Ashlee passed me the blunt.

"Call him and tell him exactly how we practiced." I unblocked Kyle's number and called him. He answered on the first ring.

"I thought I was going to have to make another trip."

"No, actually I was thinking maybe we try something different tonight," I said, exhaling the smoke from my mouth.

"I like different."

"I wanna bring a friend."

"A friend?" I could feel his excitement through the phone.

"Yeah, Leslie. I was thinking maybe the three of us could have some fun."

"Of course we can. Are you on your way?" Kyle said eagerly.

"I'm picking her up now. I should be there in 30 minutes."

"Okay, baby girl. See you then." My stomach turned hearing him call me that. I hung up the phone and smiled at Ashlee. Kadence was changing into all black like she was preparing for a mission or something. Ashlee and I both giggled.

"What?" She looked in the mirror and tucked her long hair underneath an all-black fitted cap.

"Why are you dressed like that?"

"I don't want to be seen." Kadence looked in the mirror again confused as to what Ashlee and I found so damn funny.

"Sis, it's dark as fuck, and we're in a rental car. Who's gone be checkin' for you?" Ashlee and I burst into laughter again. Kadence rolled her eyes and sat down on the bed.

"I can't stand you high bitches!" She put her shoes on. Ashlee and I had in matching lingerie. Both of our hair was pulled into a tight ponytail.

"So when we get in there, I'll follow your lead. He's gonna be more receptive to you first. I'm just there for back up." I nodded my head and took a shot. Kadence took the shot glass from me.

"Stay sober. That weed is bad enough. One mistake could fuck up everything."

"Okay, let's go." I stood to my feet.

The gun that Kadence gave me was in my purse. I took a deep breath and followed them out to the garage. Kadence planned to sit outside and wait just in case anything went wrong. Ashlee would be there if I couldn't handle the job. I was quiet the whole way there. When Kadence pulled in the driveway, my stomach was in knots.

"You sure you can handle this?" Kadence turned in her seat and stared at me.

"Yes, Kay!" I tried to hide the nervousness that was growing inside of me. I opened the door and got out. Kadence leaned her seat all the way back.

"Call me if you need me," she whispered as I walked past her. I walked up to the door and opened it. Ashlee was right behind me. I looked at her, and she nodded her head.

"Hey daddy," I called as I stepped inside. He came around the corner holding a bottle of Cristal and three wine glasses. Kyle was fine as hell. I almost forgot the reason we were here.

"Hey, baby girl." He smiled and walked over to us. He stretched his hand towards Ashlee, who shook it and smiled.

"Nice to meet you, I'm Kyle, and you are?"

"Xena," Ashlee replied quickly.

"Xena," Kyle repeated after her. "I like that name."

Ashlee smiled and took off her coat. He handed her a glass and popped the cork on the bottle. Ashlee squeaked with laughter as I took off my coat. Kyle wrapped his arms around my waist and pulled me in for a kiss. I kissed him passionately and motioned for Ashlee to look around.

"Your place is so nice, Kyle. Do you mind if I look around?" Kyle ignored her, and she walked around the house checking everywhere for anything suspicious. Kyle and I made out until Ashlee came back.

"Let's take this upstairs," I whispered in his ear. Kyle bout broke his neck climbing the stairs two at a time. I looked back at Ashlee who nodded her head for encouragement.

"You good?" she asked before we followed Kyle into the room.

"Yeah." I walked into the room and pushed Kyle onto the bed. I pulled two pairs of handcuffs from the bed.

"What are you gonna do with those?" he asked. His eyes were shining with excitement.

"I am going to make sure you can't get away." I climbed on top of him and cuffed both of his wrists to the wooden headboard. Ashlee turned on the sound bar that sat on the TV stand across from the bed.

"Temperatures rising, and you're body's yearning for me. Girl lay it on me, I place no one above thee. Oh take me to your ecstasy. It seems like you're ready!"

R. Kelly blasted through the speaker as Ashlee danced seductively in the corner. I leaned down and kissed Kyle. While he was distracted, I pointed to the closet where I knew he hid his safe. She nodded her head and walked over to the bed. She climbed on the other side of Kyle. I leaned into her and put my head into her neck. Kyle's dick instantly got hard underneath me. I nodded my head, and Ashlee climbed from the bed. She walked over to the purses and pulled both guns out. I quickly kissed Kyle before he could see what she was doing.

"I'm sorry I had to do this, but it has to end somehow," I whispered.

"Listen, it's over between Whitney and me. That's what I wanted to tell you."

"But, I've heard that before, and it was a lie then. So I'm sure it's probably a lie now." I got out of the bed and stood next to Ashlee. She moved in closer while tightened the silencer on my gun.

"What's the combo to the safe, Kyle?" she sang. Kyle frowned his face while he tried to figure out what had just happened.

"You're robbing me? Kenedee, I give you everything you ask for!" he screamed.

"What's the code and don't take all day," I said. My nerves were getting bad, and I was ready for this to be over with.

"I can identify you. This is crazy. Take these damn cuffs off of me!" I raised my pistol and pointed it at his head.

"Or maybe you won't be able to know I'm listening." Ashlee smiled at me. I walked over to the safe while she aimed her Glock at his temple.

"I'm not telling you shit! Take these cuffs off, bitch!"

"Now, I'm a bitch? See how fast these niggas flip on you?" I asked Ashlee who smacked Kyle with the butt of her gun.

"You're wasting my time, and my babysitter has to be home soon. Now run it." Blood poured from the small wound ok his head.

"The code is your birthday," Kyle said quietly. I froze in my tracks and stared at him.

"Go open the safe!" Ashlee yelled at me. I pressed my birthday into the keypad, and the door sprang open. Ashlee turned the music down and walked over to the window.

"Somebody just pulled in the driveway."

"What?" I ran to my purse and called Kadence. I saw the text from her before she answered.

Kadence: Hide, someone's here... coming in.

Ashlee put the silencer on her Glock and aimed it at the door.

"Kyle? Whose car is that?" I recognized her voice immediately.

"That's his wife," I whispered to Ashlee.

"Whit! Help I'm in—" Ashlee smacked him in the mouth with her gun.

"What the fuck are you callin' her in here for? You're already bout to die!" The door swung open, and Whitney walked in. I moved deeper into the closet.

"What is going on here?"

"Get on the bed with your husband." Ashlee turned and looked at me. All of the confidence that I had before was gone. I just knew we were about to get caught and be sent to jail. Whitney climbed next to Kyle.

"What kind of shit have you gotten yourself into now?" She eyed Ashlee with attitude all over her face.

"No talking!" Kadence walked into the room with her own gun pointed at them. She looked around the room and stood next to Ashlee.

"You should have taken my first warning." Kadence let off two shots and followed suit. I stared in shock as their lifeless bodies lumped over each other. I grabbed the stacks of cash from the safe and stuffed them into my purse.

"Where is Kenedee?" Ashlee walked over and opened the closet door.

"Hiding in the damn closet." I stood to my feet and walked out.

"I wasn't hidin'. I was emptying the safe. There's another one downstairs. He keeps the key in his wallet." Ashlee patted his pockets. Kadence walked over and looked out the window.

"I don't feel so good." She wiped the sweat from her forehead. I stared at Whitney and Kyle. I felt a sense of relief that that part of my life was over.

"Why don't y'all go outside. I'll check the other safe and be out in a second. Kadence headed out the door quickly. Ashlee followed behind her.

"You sure you're good?" I nodded my head and followed behind her.

"Yeah, I'll be right out."

I switched purses with her and made my way to Kyle's study. I opened the safe. There was even more money and jewels in this one as well as a couple of notebooks and some envelopes. I grabbed everything and put them in the bag. I started towards the door, but something stopped me. I had come to get some closure, but I didn't really feel like I got it. I dropped the bag by the front door and climbed the stairs to the bedroom. I grabbed the bottle of Cristal that we had been drinking and took a sip from the bottle. I walked over to the small bar in the bedroom. There was a box of cigars and matches next to a bottle of Hennessy and Remy. I grabbed the Henny and drenched the bed and both of their bodies with the alcohol. I untied Kyle's hands from the headboard and put a cigar in his hand. I lit the cigar and dropped the match on the bed. Smoke slowly started to fill the room. I dropped another match, and the bed caught flame. I turned and ran from the house, grabbing the bag on the way.

"What took you so long?" Kadence was leaning against the car as I came out.

"I had to do something. Let's get out of here." I looked up at the house as the smoke alarm started to ring. Kadence and I joined Ashlee in the car.

"I was almost worried about you. I see you came through though." Ashlee smiled and threw the bag over the seat.

Kadence drove to Ashlee's house in silence. Ashlee and I pulled shorts and t-shirts over our lingerie. We all got out, each one of us carrying a purse filled with cash. Ashlee unlocked the door and motioned for us to come inside.

"Mommy!" Two small boys sprang to their feet and rushed us at the door.

"Hey, guys. How were they tonight?" She turned to a small girl sitting on the couch.

"No problem at all, Mrs. Williams. Your husband called he said he would be home late, but you beat him. Dinner is on the counter," the girl rambled on as she made her way out the door. Kadence nudged me.

"You did good, kid." She smiled and wrapped her arm around my shoulder. I don't know what made me happier; the fact that she was proud, or knowing that we had made so much money and had gotten Whitney and Kyle out of my life.

"Come on y'all."

We followed Ashlee down to the floor. She opened the door to a small room with a card table, a small TV, and a recliner in it. She dumped the contents of the purse she had on the table. I did the same. Kadence walked over and sat in the recliner.

"I'm gonna take a nap. Wake me up when y'all done." She raised her feet and closed her eyes. Ashlee and I divided the bills into equal piles of one hundred dollars.

"How much you get?" Ashlee asked as I counted the last stack.

"$8,700." Kadence sat up from her chair.

"You got eight racks from that safe?" I nodded my head.

I opened the envelopes and read the papers, which were deeds to a bunch of properties that the two of them owned. The last envelope in the pile caught my attention. It was the only one that was yellow instead of white. It had a K on the back under the flap. I pulled the papers from the envelope and read them. There was a deed a condominium in my name, a bank statement with an available balance of $10,000, and a separation agreement that needed only Whitney's signature. A tear fell from my eye as I realized what I had just done. Kyle was going to leave Whitney. That's why she was there to sign the papers in front of me.

"Ken? What's wrong?" She ran across the room and snatched the papers from my hand.

"Oh shit!" Kadence dropped to her knees and wrapped her arms around me.

"What? What does this mean?" Ashlee held the papers and stared at us.

"He was leaving his wife. He made sure Kenedee would be good during the process."

"Damn." Ashlee turned on the TV and lit the blunt. "I don't know how to make you feel better, sis." She passed the blunt to me. "But, I got a lot of this shit here. You can smoke yourself to sleep." She smiled and shrugged her shoulders. I smiled back and took the blunt.

"Thanks, Ash." I let the smoke fill my lungs. Ashlee turned to the news while Kadence split the money in half.

"Where's your cut?"

"I don't want it. I just wanted to make sure you were ready for whatever the hell you agreed to with Jazelle."

"Do you think I made a mistake?" Kadence stopped what she was doing and stared at me.

"It doesn't matter at this point. Love is a dangerous game, Ken. You can't take this shit lightly. What's done is done."

"Oh shit!" Ashlee said and turned the volume up on the TV. "You burned the house down?" She stared at me. Kadence looked down at me as well.

"You set a fire, Ken?" She focused on the newscaster.

"It appears that the fire started in the bedroom where the Mr. Hughes fell asleep smoking. There were no survivors. We'll keep you updated as the firefighters struggle to tame this fire. It has already spread to the neighboring houses. They have both been evacuated."

The news switched to the weather, and they both stared at me. Kadence pulled me into a hug and whispered, "It's okay, sis. I got you forever." I cried into her shirt. "Let's get out of here." She packed up my half and the paperwork and smiled at Ashlee.

"Thanks for your help."

"No problem. I'm always down for a girl's night out." She gave us both hugs and walked us to the door. "Call me if you need to talk. Sometimes it's easier to talk to strangers."

I nodded my head and got in the car. I didn't want to talk to anyone. Right now, I just wanted sleep.

14

KADENCE

It was the morning of Loyal's memorial service. To be honest, it was the furthest thing from my mind after the shit that went down last night. Kenedee hadn't said a single word since we left Ashlee's house. It was early, but I wanted to make breakfast for my family. I went down to the kitchen to find mama already up and cutting potatoes.

"Good morning, mama. How'd you sleep?" I loved having my mama here. It felt normal, as opposed to the drastic turn my life had taken in the last few weeks.

"I slept fine. How are you doing? Did you decide if you were going to the service or not?" I poured myself a glass of orange juice.

"I will if Kai wants to. She was still up in the air about it yesterday."

"Well, I'll make an appearance if you don't feel the up to it."

That was one of the main reasons I loved my mama. She was annoying 80% of the time, but with that other 20%, she did whatever she had to, to keep her children from any type of harm, and I admired her for that. Some people weren't so lucky.

"Thank you, mama." I pulled the ingredients to make omelets for everyone.

"I'm going to go home tonight, Kadence." I turned and stared at her. I was sure she would be safe at home, but I wanted her here with me.

"But mama, what if something else happens."

"What if it does? I can't stay here forever. Bryson wants his woman back before your head starts to spin." Mama laughed and walked over to me.

"I can take care of myself, Kay. Who you think taught you?"

I smiled, but I was still upset. Bryson was keeping me out of the loop on everything. Mama and I continued to make breakfast in silence. It wasn't long before the family joined us.

"Morning, mommy." Kai bounced into the kitchen. Bryson was right behind her. "Uncle B and I are going fishing." I looked up at them both, confused.

"Fishing?" Bryson kissed me on the cheek and smiled.

"Yeah, fishing. Why you look so surprised?" I flipped Kai's omelet and turned to face them.

"I just didn't see you as a fishing kind of guy."

"I'm a jack of all trades, baby. You ain't know?" Bryson took a seat next to Kai. The two of them whispered and giggled until I bought their plates.

"Mommy, you wanna go fishing?" Fishing was not something I felt confident doing, but for Kai, I would do anything.

"Sure why not."

"You have to hook your own worm. Uncle B said he's not helping us." I laughed and looked at Bryson who had a huge grin on his face. I mouthed the words thank you to him and he nodded his head.

Kenedee had not come out of her room yet. I made her a plate of food and went up the hall to the guest room she was staying in. I knocked on the door and let myself in. Kenedee had papers thrown all over the bed. Her hair was piled wildly on the top of her head. She had her glasses hanging from the tip of her nose.

"Hey Ken, I brought you breakfast."

"I wasn't the only one," she said quickly flipping through the notebooks on her bed. "He had books full of bitches he was taking care of— Paris being one of them!" She shoved the notebook in my face. I took the book and handed her the plate.

"His niece, Paris?"

"That ain't his damn niece. She is literally just another thot on the list." Kenedee started eating. "That nigga had this shit down to a science. Each girl had a code, and he recorded everything." I could see she was feeling completely different from the way she was a few hours earlier.

"Well, it's good you did what you did then." Kenedee nodded her head.

"I'm gonna sale the condo, close the accounts, and move the fuck on. I wasted too much of my life with them people." I heard the doorbell ringing followed by Kai running through the house.

"Mommy! The police are here for you." Kenedee's face was pale.

"Just relax. Stay here your face alone says you're guilty of something." A lumped started to form in my throat. I took my time walking up the hall. I turned the corner and saw the detective that had called me in for questioning in Loyal's murder.

"Hello Mrs. Jackson, how are you?"

"I'm getting better every day. How can I help you?" He looked around the room. Everyone was staring at him.

"Uh, have you seen your sister?" My heart felt like it would leap out of my chest.

"Which one?" I said as calmly as I could.

"Jazelle. I went back to question her, but I couldn't find her."

"A few days ago. I could call her if you want," I offered. He shook his head and smiled.

"As long as she didn't skip town." He chuckled and glanced around the room again. I stared at Bryson who pulled out his phone.

"No, sir. I doubt that she would do a thing like that." I forced a smile. In the back of my head, I didn't know what the fuck Jazelle would and wouldn't do anymore. It was very possible her ass was in another country by now.

"Well, if you hear from her, tell her to give me a call." He handed me his card and headed towards the door.

"I sure will. Is she a suspect in my husband's murder?" I moved closer and whispered to him in case Kai was listening.

"Not right now."

"Well, are you all any closer to finding who did this?" He opened the door and stepped out on the porch.

"I don't know how to say this delicately, but your husband was not a well-liked man. There are many people who wanted him dead." I gasped and covered my mouth.

"I just don't understand how things got so bad for him," I cried. "Loyal was the one person I was certain would never hurt me."

"You would be surprised at what goes on in a person's mind, especially when fame and drugs are involved."

"Drugs?"

"Yes, ma'am. Even though he hadn't been released from the jail that long, his toxicology report was unusually high."

"That's odd."

"Why is it odd?"

"I thought he was trying to get clean is all." He put his hand on my shoulder and smiled weakly.

"I apologize. I know this is already a hard time for you."

"No, it's fine. Please just keep me updated." He nodded his head and walked away. I waited for him to get in his car and drive off. I immediately tried to call Jazelle, but her number had been disconnected

What the fuck is this bitch doing? I asked myself and walked back in the house. Kenedee had joined everyone else in the kitchen.

"Did Jazelle call you?" I turned to her. She shook her head and sat down at the table without saying anything.

"Kadence let me talk to you for a second."

Bryson walked over and grabbed my hand. He pulled me into the bedroom that we shared. Bryson closed the door and locked it behind him. He led me to the bed and sat down beside me.

"How are you feeling today?"

"I'm good, baby how are you?" Bryson stared at me like he was trying to see if I was lying or not.

"As long as you're good, I'm good. You ready to go fishing?"

"Actually, I think I'm going to go find Jazelle. I don't know what the hell she got going on, but it's weird even for her."

"Yeah, something's going on."

"You've been over there?" I asked, feeling slightly jealous that he even had to be involved. Bryson smiled and kissed my forehead.

"Don't be like that, baby." Bryson planted kisses all over my face and neck. I laid back on the bed. Bryson instantly spread my legs and kissed from my feet to the edge of my boy shorts.

"Everybody is here, B. They're going to hear us."

"I guess you better be quiet then."

He planted the same small kisses up the center of my panties. My pussy started throbbing. Bryson snatched my underwear off and threw them on the floor: He didn't waste any time devouring me like his life depended on him. Me being quiet went out the window as soon as Bryson put his tongue to work.

"Beeeeee!" I moaned and locked my fingers in dreads.

"You taste so fuckin' good, Kay," Bryson said in between his attempts to snatch my soul. Bryson spit on his index and middle finger and slid them inside me while slurping on my pussy. Any and everything that was bothering me before was a distant memory now.

"Stop fighting me." Bryson gripped my thighs tighter. I did exactly as I was told and let go of everything I had in me.

"Damn, girl." Bryson got up and laughed. "I ain't say try to drown me." He licked his lips and walked into the bathroom. I laid there trying to catch my breath. Bryson came back and sat down beside me.

"Are you stress-free now?" He rubbed my belly with a smile on his face. Even though I wasn't that far in, this pregnancy was totally different from Kai. All I wanted to do was eat and sleep, but as usual, I was running behind my sisters trying to fix their messes.

"Yes. I feel great." I grabbed both sides of his face and kissed him. There was a knock at the door. Bryson went to answer it while I rolled over and turned on the news.

"Is it safe to come in here?" Kenedee asked, covering her eyes with her hands.

"Yeah, it's safe. Why wouldn't it be?" Kenedee moved her hand and looked up at Bryson.

"First off, y'all nasty. Second, Kai wants to know if you're ready." Bryson laughed and walked out the room.

"You okay, Ken?" I asked still unable to move.

"Yeah." She was staring at the TV.

"Did they say they had any leads about the Hughes?"

"No. I just turned it on. Don't worry, Ken. Everything will be fine. I always got you, don't I?" She nodded her head and stared at the TV screen. The reporter repeated the information that we already knew.

"Do you think they'll find out it was us?" I shook my head and wrapped my half-naked body in a sheet from the bed.

"No, they won't. I'm going to take a shower, and then we can go get pedicures."

Kenedee nodded her head and slowly walked towards the door. I knew my sister wasn't made for this life, and it pissed me off that Jazelle even brought it up, especially if she was going to fucking disappear.

I took my time getting dressed after my shower. The house was quiet, which had become unusual in the past couple of days. I walked through the house, and just like I suspected, everyone was gone. Right when I was about to pull out my phone, Kenedee walked through the door.

"Mama wanted to go home. She thought if we waited, you would talk her out of it." I nodded my head because she was right. I grabbed my purse and slid my sunglasses over my eyes. Going out in public had been a hassle ever since the news of Loyal and what he had done broke.

"You drive, I pay?" Kenedee nodded her head and walked out on the porch. She stopped dead in her tracks.

"Who is that?" I asked, following her stare. A huge grin spread across her face as the guy climbed out of the work van with a bouquet of white roses.

"Hey Ms. Kenedee, how are you?" The smile was still there as she ran down the front stairs.

"Hey, Zane! I didn't think I would see you again." She jumped into his arms, while I scratched my head trying to figure out who the hell he was and how he knew where I lived. Zane put Kenedee down and handed her the flowers. He handed a smaller bouquet to me and smiled.

"Hello Mrs. Jackson, glad to see you're doing better. I'm Zane. I remodeled your floor for you."

"Oh, thank you. You did a wonderful job. How do you know my sister?" I asked. Kenedee was still grinning, and I had never seen her smile like that before.

"She called me for this job. I couldn't stop thinking about her, so I decided to come back and shoot my shot."

"Shoot your shot?"

"It means mind your business." Kenedee stepped in and cut him off. Zane laughed, and I could see why Kenedee was on him the way that she was. He was cute with deep dimples and pearly white teeth, which was more than you could ask for these days.

"Want to go to lunch?" Kenedee nodded her head.

"Mind if we reschedule, Kay?" She was already headed to the van. It didn't matter what I said either way.

"Have fun, Ken. Be careful."

I watched Zane help Kenedee into his van. Not wanting to be home alone, I got in my car and drove to the nail shop. Just because Kenedee didn't want to go, didn't mean I couldn't pamper myself.

15

JAZELLE

It was almost four a.m. when Royce walked in the room waking me up. It was clear that something had him shook.

"Jazzy! Baby? We gotta go." He was going through the drawers, throwing my clothes into garbage bags.

"What is going on?" I asked, but I may as well have not even been in the room. "Royce!" I clapped my hands, and he turned and stared at me.

"We have to get out of here." I turned on the overhead light and examined him. His clothes were wrinkled and dirty. His face had dried up blood around his mouth and snot around his nose.

"Please just talk to me. Tell me what is going on!"

"Some shit went down with my wife's brother. He's probably on his way here now. So, we need to leave." I snatched the bag holding my belongings from him.

"Did you say your wife?" Royce snapped out of whatever trace he was in and snatched me up by my neck. Royce stared me in my eyes. He squeezed until I thought I would pass out. As quickly as he has snatched me up, he dropped my ass on the floor.

"I said let's fuckin' go!" I grabbed a pair of UW sweat pants and pulled a red tank top over my head. Royce grabbed the garbage bags and ran outside. I followed him slightly scared by what would happen next.

"We need money. You know who got some?" I ignored his question, trying to figure out how I had even gotten myself in this situation. Royce raised his hand and backhanded me across my face.

"Pay attention! Do you know who has some?" I nodded my head and mumbled the address to the one person I knew I could always depend on.

I knew that Mama Lena was staying with Kadence. I figured I could hit her stash, get what I needed, and be gone before anyone even knew what happened. Royce turned off the lights and pulled into the driveway. He unhooked his seatbelt, but I stopped him.

"It'll be faster if I go alone." Royce frowned and checked himself in the sun visor mirror.

"You don't want to introduce me to the fam?" I was more scared of what may happen to my mama if Royce had another one of his fits in front of her.

"It's not that, babe. Just give me a few minutes."

I got out the car and pulled my hoodie over my head. I grabbed the spare key that Mama Lena had always kept underneath the mat at the back door. I opened the door and stepped inside the dark house. I made my way to Mama Lena's bedroom. The house was silent. I went to her closet and moved the floorboard. I heard footsteps in the front of the house as I stuffed the money into my hoodie pocket.

"Jazzy? Is that you?" The light came on, and Mama Lena stood in the doorway behind me.

"Mama? What are you doing here?" I struggled to get the floorboard back into place.

"What are you doing, Jazelle?"

"I'm sorry, Mama Lena. I need this money right now." Mama Lena's face held more hurt than my heart could take.

"Jazelle, baby what is going on? You know I can help you."

"I don't need no help, mama. Right now all I need is this money." I tried to push past her, but she wouldn't budge.

"Jazelle?"

"Move!" I shoved her out of the way a little harder than I expected. She fell to the floor with a thud. I stepped over her and ran out of the back door. Royce was doing a line in the car.

"Let's go." Royce finished what he had started before he pulled off. "We need to go Royce! Put that shit away!"

Royce backed out of the driveway as Mama Lena opened the front door. She clutched her elbow and locked eyes with me. I mouthed the words "I'm sorry" as we faded into the darkness.

"What's wrong with you?" Royce asked.

"You mean aside from all of the bullshit you're getting me into?" I snapped. Seeing the pain in Mama Lena's face did something to me. It was harder to shake than I thought it would be. Royce handed me the golden straw that now gave him the ability to control me.

"Where are we going, Royce?" I asked as I tried to make myself feel better. It was only a matter of time before Mama Lena told Kenedee or Kadence what happened and I would have to fight one of those bitches.

"We're just going to get out of town for a few days. Is that okay with you?" I slowly nodded my head, the drugs starting to take effect. I pulled my cell phone from my pocket and threw it out the window. Kadence had brought me down enough. The way I see it, she deserved everything she had coming to her. She had everybody fooled into thinking she was this goody two shoes when in reality she is a stone cold killer. All over the world, people were bashing Loyal for what he did to her. All the while not knowing, what she had done to him. I leaned my head back. My nose was starting to run.

"Baby, why don't you get daddy right real quick."

I rolled my eyes and unbuckled my seat belt. Royce was already unbuttoning his pants and pulling his dick out. It amazed me how fast niggas could get ready to get some head, but ask a nigga to take out the garbage, and it may take a year! As much bad that Royce had brought into my life, his dick made everything worth it. I massaged his dick and slid it in my mouth. Royce moaned loudly.

"Damn Jazzy! You been holding back on a nigga?" I nodded my head while relaxing my throat.

My thoughts turned to Bryson and how good it used to be when he was taking me down. Royce was good, but he ain't have nothing on King B. I fantasize that Bryson and I were riding through the country, on our way to a special date he had planned especially for me.

"Damn baby! Slow down." Royce moaned, but it only made me go harder. Imagining that he was Bryson had me making Royce my bitch. Royce swerved down the highway, moaning my name. His phone started to ring. Before he could answer, I saw the name *wifey* pop up on the screen.

"Who was that?" I asked, stroking his dick with both of my hands.

"Nobody." Royce was struggling to focus on the road.

"If it's nobody, why won't you answer it?" I flicked my tongue across the tip of his dick.

Royce's phone started ringing again. I sucked on his balls and felt the car jerk hard. I sat up and stared out the window. I could tell by the way his dick was throbbing that Royce was about to come."

"Answer your phone." I snatched it from his hand and pressed the answer key. I put the phone on speaker handed it back to Royce. "Say hello," I instructed as I took him in my mouth.

"Hello?"

"Where the fuck are you, Royce? Got these niggas in here fucking up my damn house!" The woman screamed on the other end of the phone.

"Man, I can't talk about that now."

"You can't talk? This motherfucka said he can't talk. You got me fucked up, Royce. These niggas in here threatening me and our kids and you telling me you can't talk right now?" I stopped what I was doing and stared at Royce.

"You have kids?"

"Who was that?" the woman asked quickly. "I knooow you're not with a bitch right now?" Royce pulled over on the shoulder and covered my mouth.

"Tee, stop buggin' ain't nobody gone do nothin'. I'm over here getting the money now." Hearing those words hurt worse than anything that Royce had done to me thus far.

"You know what? You're a dead man. I know how to find you and that bitch you fucking!" She ended the call.

"FUCK!" Royce yelled. "Why did you do that?" He head-butted me and my head flew into the window. Royce punched me in my mouth. "You had to open your big ass mouth. Royce jumped from the car and ran around to the other side. He opened the door and snatched me from the car by my dreads. Royce kicked me in my side.

"I'm sorry," I mumbled in between kicks to my body. He walked off cursing about how stupid I was. I jumped back in the car and locked the doors. I slid into the driver's seat and buckled my seatbelt. Royce knocked on the passenger window.

"Jazzy, baby, open the door. I'm sorry I hit you." I put the car in drive and slowly pulled away. Royce tapped on the window harder. "Open this fuckin' door!" he screamed.

I stepped on the gas and peeled off leaving him on the side of the road. After I had driven enough that I knew I would not be able to burst my window, I stopped and looked at myself in the mirror. I looked horrible. Bruised and bloody, I did a U-turn and drove back to where I had left Royce. He was standing in the middle of the street trying to get reception. I turned off the lights and crept up on him. Royce turned around and walked towards the car. I waited until he was close and slammed on the gas pedal. Royce grunted and rolled over the entire car. I stopped when I saw him rolled over the back window and past the truck. I did another U-Turn and rolled over his body like a speed bump. My mind was racing, and so was my heart. I didn't know what to do, so I followed my first mind and continued on the highway. I didn't know if Royce had survived, but I honestly didn't care. He had caused enough pain in my life, and I was over it. A wife and kids was the final straw.

I drove to Milwaukee. I didn't know where I was headed, but I knew Madison needed to be in my rearview for the moment. I pulled over and counted the money I had taken from Mama Lena. It was a little over $900. That woman never believed in using a bank, and maybe this incident would help change her mind. I planned to pay her everything back, but first I needed to get my mind right. I clutched the locket that she gave me a few years ago and prayed that she would forgive me.

16

BRYSON

I pulled up to the warehouse and saw Bruce standing out front. It was late, so the cold air had set in. I got out of the car and shook up with him.

"Braylon's inside already?" Bruce nodded his head. I wasn't in the mood to deal with his spoiled ass today, so I kept walking until I saw Braylon sitting at a table covered in coke and dollar bills.

"Whassup man? What was so important that I had to leave my girl this late?"

"Stop bitchin'. From what I hear your girl got more heart than you anyway." Braylon laughed.

"Fuck you, bruh." I smiled. Kadence did have heart, but she wasn't fuckin' with me. Braylon stood up as Bruce walked in.

"Watch this." Braylon stared at Bruce. "Don't move from this fuckin' spot until I get back."

Bruce mumbled something under his breath and sat down at the table. Braylon motioned for me to follow him into a different section of the building. He pulled out a set of keys and unlocked the door.

"What you live here or something, nigga?"

"Mind ya' business." He walked inside and turned on the light.

There was somebody slumped in a chair in the middle of the room. He had a black cotton pillowcase tied tightly around his head.

"Who the fuck is that?" Braylon walked over and kicked the chair from under him.

"What you want lil' nigga?"

"Kadence," he whimpered, struggling to get free. I looked at Braylon and took a step closer to him.

"Fuck you want with Kadence?"

"I ain't telling you shit until you let me go."

"I ain't letting you go until you tell me what I need to know. We can do this all night, my nigga." I turned back to Braylon. "Where you find this nigga?"

"Outside your girl's spot," Braylon said and stared at the covered man.

"Is that you, B? You did this shit to me?" I looked over at Braylon, and he stared back at me his hand already on his pistol. I snatched the pillowcase from his head and stared Zee in the eyes.

"What the fuck are you still doing here?"

"Kadence fuckin' owes me, man."

"Bruh, whatever issue you had is dead, and if it ain't, you need to dead it before you end up dead."

"Fuck you and that bitch." I laughed.

"I don't think you understand the position you're in, my nigga." Zee spit in my face. I pulled my Glock from my jeans and held it to his head. "Are you really ready to die for another man's shit?" Zee looked back and forth between Braylon and me.

"Fuck y'all niggas. Them bitches had more heart than y'all." Braylon burst out laughing.

"Told you, bro." However, I ain't see shit funny. I emptied the clip and walked away.

"Next time don't wake me up for no bullshit."

I walked back to the truck. Last time we met, I told Zee that Kadence was off limits. Whatever she owed him would be given back when he fuckin' left town. Now this motherfucka had me doing shit I said I wouldn't go back to. Bruce was still sitting at the table when I walked past. He was so interested in his phone that he didn't even see me coming.

"You supposed to be paying attention, fool." Bruce looked up at me with an attitude.

"I am nigga. I heard your big ass feet."

"You got a problem with me?" I asked him, squaring up across the table.

"Naw big bro, other than the fact that you should be thanking me for saving your bitch and a bunch of other things; nothing at all." I reached across the table and smacked him in the mouth.

"Watch your mouth when you talk about the mother of my child." Bruce jumped across the table, tackling me to the ground. We wrestled back and forth until Braylon came out and pulled us apart.

"It's a fuckin' body back here and y'all dumbasses out here fighting?" Braylon blew his cigar smoke in my face. "What the fuck is the problem?" Bruce was breathing hard and lookin' at me like he wanted to make a move.

"Bryson acts like somebody supposed to bow down to him and his bitch!" he spat on the ground in my direction. I pushed Braylon out the way and pulled Bruce into a headlock.

"What the fuck I say?" The longer I held him, the more pissed off he got. Bruce always thought he was the toughest nigga around, but he wasn't. A few years ago, the lick that Braylon and I hit was initially a lick that Bruce came across.

I HAD JUST finished smoking and was dozing off on the couch when Bruce burst in the door. He was dragging one of the suitcases with wheels and had a duffle bag damn near bigger than him draped across his body.

"Are you moving or something?"

"Bryson, I need your help. Help me hide this before mama comes home." I got up and took the bag from his shoulder.

"I'll put this in my room; slide that under your bed." I looked at Bruce, and he was clearly shook.

"We can't hide it here. We need another spot."

"Bruce, what's in here man?" I unzipped the bag and looked inside. There was a whole lot of money. "Where'd you get this?"

"I took it." I looked at Bruce. I wanted to know more, but first, we needed to get this shit out of here. I knew having this much money only meant one thing was in the other bag.

"Who you take it from?"

"It don't matter! Are you gone help me or not?" Bruce turned back to the door.

"Yeah, I'll help you, but you gone have to tell me something. Go put it in your room." Bruce did what he was told and took a shower.

I waited until everyone was sleep and dumped the bags into ten garbage bags. I buried the bags in the huge garden that my mother had been asking for. The next morning I planted seeds that I knew would come in handy for the neighborhood. I told Bruce that I had taken care of everything and I would give it back when it was safe to bring it out. Later that day, Duke came and tried to kill my little brother in my mother's house, in front of my mother. That was also the day I caught my first body. I walked in and saw Bruce on his knees pleading for his life.

"Where my shit, lil' nigga?" Duke growled. He had a gun pointed at Bruce and my mama.

"I told you I ain't got it."

"You do! And I'm tired of asking for it." He cocked the pistol that was pointed at Bruce. I was standing behind him. Bruce saw me, but Duke did not.

"Man, I don't know who lied to you. I ain't take shit from you."

Duke pulled the trigger and hit the mirror behind Bruce. Mama screamed and dropped to the floor begging Duke to spare her baby boy. I pulled the gun that Braylon had given me for safety from my pants and cocked the trigger behind his ear.

"Drop your gun, my mans. My brother damn sure ain't gone be the one to die."

Duke started at me in the mirror. I could see it in his face he was wondering how the hell I snuck up on him. Duke raised his gun and pointed it at Bruce. Feeling nervous, I pulled the trigger. His head burst open and blood and brain matter splattered all over the both of us. Bruce still in his knees looked up at me.

"You saved my life?" I helped him to his feet.

"Why wouldn't I?" I looked over at mama who was still frozen. "Ma, I'm sorry."

"Sorry for what?" She was calmer now than I had ever heard her before. "I told you, you always take care of your little brother, no matter what. I meant that shit." She took the gun from my hands. "Take those clothes off and get in the shower, both of you." Mama frowned at us and pulled a garbage bag from under the kitchen cabinet. "Put everything in here." She walked over to the house phone and called someone.

"I need you to call Rez and get him here now." She hung up the phone and turned back to Bruce and I. "Go! Now!" Mama screamed.

I threw my clothes into the garbage bag and ran up the stairs to the bathroom. My heart was beating way faster than it should have been. I scrubbed my body with that fruity shit that mama always told us never to touch.

When I came out, Bruce was sitting on my bed.

"I need that bag. I gotta get out of here."

"It's too hot right now. You don't think motherfuckas finna be out here looking for Duke?"

"I know they are, and that's why I need to move around." Bruce stood in front of me with his chest puffed out.

"You feelin' some type of way, nigga?"

"Why? You gone murk me too?" Bruce stared me down. I stepped into my jeans and moved close to him.

"Get the fuck out!" Bruce shoved me so hard that I flew into the mirror above the dresser. Mama came in with Braylon and my Uncle Rez and pulled us apart.

"Tell Bryson he ain't my damn daddy! Don't nobody fuckin need him!"

"Shut yo' bitch ass up! You needed me a few minutes ago!" I muffed him and pulled my shirt over my head. "Matter of fact, y'all don't need me. Watch out; I'm gone." I pushed Bruce to the side and kissed mama on her cheek.

That was the day I moved out my mama's house. The next morning,

Braylon found the bags in the yard and split them between the two of us. Bruce never forgave me for not telling Braylon that it was his stash. I didn't give a fuck. When you steal from people you always gotta remember that that makes you a target as well. Better us than a nigga on the street.

I LOOSENED the grip I had on his neck until he calmed down.

"I'm still your big brother, don't ever disrespect me."

I turned and walked out of the warehouse. I was putting in more work for Kadence than I had ever put in for myself. I drove back to the house. It was pitch black inside and out. I pulled into the driveway and started to roll. I knew that the smell of smoke bothered Kadence, so I tried to stay outside for the most part. The music on my phone stopped, and it started to vibrate. I almost ignored it, but with all the action that had been going on lately, I decided against it.

"Yo?"

"Bryson? I need your help." Jazelle's voice was low. I could tell she was fighting back tears.

"What's going on? Where you been?" I could hear her breathing hard.

"I fucked up, B. I really fucked up." She repeated over and over.

"Where are you?"

"Please don't tell Kadence." She hung up the phone. A few seconds later the notification with Jazelle's location popped up.

"Milwaukee, Jazzy?" I started the car and made my way to her. I texted Kadence so she wouldn't worry when she woke up.

I made a run with Braylon. Be back later.

I knew she would be pissed, but hopefully, Jazelle wouldn't make me regret it.

17

KENEDEE

Zane took me out to eat and back to his place.

"How's everything been going?" he asked as he made us drinks at the bar. I watched his every move as he mixed the liquor from different bottles. I thought about what had been going on in my life in the few weeks since I had seen him last.

"Nothing much. Just livin' life. How you been?" Zane handed me a glass. If I hadn't watched him mix it myself, I would have sworn it was some kind of fruit juice instead of liquor.

"I've been thinking about you. Sick because I didn't know how to reach you." He flashed that smile that instantly made my panties wet.

"Really? What you been thinking." Zane picked me up and sat me on the bar. I took another sip from my glass. Zane stood between my legs and smiled at me.

"I think I should make you mine." He kissed my cheek gently. "What you think about that?" Zane kissed my other cheek and stared at me like he wanted to take me down right there.

"I think that could be a possibility."

My phone started to ring. It was an unknown caller. I pressed ignore and flipped my phone over on the counter. I pulled Zane closer and kissed him. Whatever was in that drink had my pussy throbbing. Zane was going to be a great stress reliever. I slid my fingers up and down his muscular arms. Zane kissed my neck as he fumbled with the button on my jeans. I pushed his hands away and jumped off the bar. I wiggled out of my jeans when I turned around Zane was staring at my body with his mouth open.

"Damn, you so sexy." He smacked my ass and bent me over the bar.

Zane planted kisses down my back. He traced the outline of my panties with his tongue before spreading my cheeks and sucking on my pussy from behind. Zane clapped my ass cheeks against his face while he swirled his tongue around my clit. I gripped the counter and braced myself for the nut I knew was coming soon. Zane spit on his fingers and slid them in and out of me while he continued to suck on my clit. I came all over his face. Zane wasted no time diving inside me. I gripped the counter harder this time. I could literally feel his dick in my stomach. Zane smacked my ass again and pulled me down on his lap. My feet dangled from the bar stool as I tried to find something to give me some kind of leverage. I wrapped my legs around Zane's waist and rode his dick like one of those lil' bitty dudes that rode the horses at the track.

"Damn, Ken! You feel so good." I gripped his dick with my pussy walls and leaned forward. Zane loudly moaned as he gripped my hips. My phone started to vibrate across the counter, but I ignored it.

"Who's blowing you up?"

"Nobody important," I moaned as I came on his dick. Zane dug his nails in my hips and came with me.

I climbed off of the stool and walked to the bathroom. While using the bathroom, I scanned the room. The more I paid attention to Zane's apartment, the more I got the feeling that he didn't live there alone. The big red flag was the hot pink and leopard print bonnet hanging on the back of the door, and the lace teddy draped over the shower curtain. I washed between my legs and walked back to the kitchen where Zane was checking his messages.

"That was dope!" He smiled and wrapped his arms around my waist.

"Yeah, it was." I debated if I should bring the items in the bathroom up. I decided against it and started to get dressed.

"Wait, where are you going? I thought we were gone chill." I shook my head and started to get dressed.

"Naw, I have to get home." Zane turned and blocked my path.

"What did I do?" He stared at me, and I wanted to forget everything that I had seen, but then, my thoughts drifted to Whitney and Kyle and the mess I had just freed myself from.

"You didn't do anything." I cupped the side of his face. "I just have to go." Zane chuckled and leaned against the desk.

"Don't tell me you're one of them hit and quit it type girls." I tried to move past him, but he kept blocking my way.

"Who lives here with you?" Zane looked confused.

"Don't nobody live here with me. This is my house." I grabbed his hand and took him to the bathroom.

"You're telling me that's your shit?" I pointed at the lingerie hanging above our heads. "Because if it is, we need to be having a completely different conversation." Zane looked up at the teddy and then back at me.

"That's my sister's..."

"And she was doing laundry here," I finished his sentence for him. Zane looked like he had just been busted.

"Okay, let me explain."

"Don't worry about it. We're good." I turned and walked out of his apartment.

It wasn't until the cold hit my body that I remembered I didn't drive. I sent for an Uber. I checked my phone, but the calls were restricted. Whoever it was would have to call straight through.

When I finally made it to Kadence's house, she was up and sitting in the living room watching TV.

"Hey, lil' nasty! Where you been all night?"

"Minding my business, nosey. What are you doing up?" I sat down on the couch next to her and grabbed a handful of her popcorn.

"Waiting on Bryson to come home." I checked the time on my phone. It was early morning— way too early for Bryson to not be home.

"Where is he?" Kadence shrugged her shoulders and rolled her eyes.

"I don't know, but he better not be where I think he is." Not wanting to upset her, I changed the subject.

"Let me see your nails." Kadence showed off the same French manicure that she always got. Kadence was a creature of habit. She did the same thing every day and got an attitude if her schedule got thrown off. "Those are cute."

"Unlike that big ass hickey on your neck. Who still gives hickeys in 2017?" I laughed and tried to cover the spot she was talking about.

"I thought you were minding your business." I looked out the window and saw someone moving through the bushes in the early morning light. "Looks like your boo is home." Kadence was off the couch and on her way to the door in a matter of seconds. I stood to go get myself cleaned up, until I saw Kadence backing away from the door with her hands in the air.

"Where the fuck is Kenedee?" I recognized Paris's voice immediately.

"Paris? This is getting borderline crazy." I turned the corner to see her pointing a gun at Kadence. "What are you doing?"

"I know you fuckin' killed him! I know you did!" she screamed, shaking the Ruger at us.

"Killed who?" I pretended not to know who she was talking about.

"My fiancé!" Kadence frowned and looked over at me.

"Paris, you buggin' boo. I didn't even know you had a fiancé. Just put the gun down." Paris was a crying mess. Her makeup was smeared and her nose was running.

"Kyle! You killed him. I know you did. I have his phone. You were the last person he talked to." I glanced at Kadence who was focused on what Paris was saying.

"I thought Kyle was your uncle." She shook her head and moved closer to me.

"He was my fucking fiancé and you took him away from me." I looked at Kadence who shrugged her shoulders.

"What kind of sick and twisted shit y'all got going on?" I took a step further into the house. Since the incident with Loyal, Bryson had booby trapped this house to have a weapon everywhere you turned. Kadence and I had the same idea. As I moved closer to the coffee table, she moved closer to the table in the foyer.

"Stop fucking moving!" Paris screamed and let a shot off in to the ceiling. Kadence sprang into action and tackled her to the ground. I snatched the gun from her hands and pointed it at her. I kicked Paris in her mouth.

"Really bitch? You gone fire a gun in my sister's house, knowing she's got a kid?" I kicked her again. Kadence pinned Paris to the ground while I grabbed the vase from the table in the foyer and smashed it over her head.

"Where is Kai?" I asked once Paris stopped moving. Kadence struggled to her feet and ran towards the stairs. I felt like my heart would beat out of my chest, waiting for her to come back. Paris was stretched out on the floor. A small pool of blood was running from her head.

"Paris, what the fuck are you doing? Like for real?" When she still didn't move I kicked her and rolled her over to her side. Paris moaned and slowly opened her eyes.

"What happened?" she asked, holding her head.

"You came in here and lost your motherfuckin' mind!" I pointed the gun at her. "Explain yourself, now." Paris took a deep breath and stared at me in silence. Kadence returned with her .9mm cocked and ready to go.

"Last time you came here, you were warned not to come back. Now you're here again for reasons I don't understand, nor do I care about." I looked back and forth between Kadence and Paris.

"Kyle and I have been messing around for a little over a year and a half. Around the same time you got kicked out of school."

"So, you've been out here stalking your boyfriend's girlfriend?" Kadence asked her gun still ready.

"I was not stalking her. Kyle asked me to keep a close eye on Kenedee because she had valuable information that could make us lose everything, so I did. It wasn't until I got close with Whitney that I found out the real truth. I figured the way things were going, the two of you would take each other out. But of course, it didn't work like that. Kyle called me and told me that he was leaving Whitney. That she was coming over to sign the divorce papers and to meet him there after because he had something important to tell me. Imagine my fuckin' surprise when I saw you leaving out and them dead."

She looked at Kadence, whose finger was twitching. My stomach was in knots. I glanced at Kadence who was staring at Paris.

"Who else did you tell?" I moved closer to her. "Or did you think you would just come over here and take us out?" Paris' eyes grew wide.

"Mommy?" Kai called from the top of the stairs.

"Yeah, baby?" Kadence backed towards the stairs with the gun still pointed at Paris.

"Who else did you fuckin' tell?" I said a little louder this time. My palms had begun to sweat. I felt like I would throw up at any second. I contemplated my next move.

"Nobody." I shook my head.

"Naw, you gotta be smarter than that, baby girl. Who knows you're here?" I watched as fear set into her face. To be honest, I kind of made me feel powerful, having someone afraid of little of me. The image of Kyle and Whitney flashed in my head as I pulled the trigger, putting a bullet in the middle of Paris's forehead. She fell to the floor. I pulled out my phone and called Zane.

"Hey, I know a way you can make it up to me if you really want to fuck with me." Zane was quiet for a few seconds. I silently prayed that he would take the bait because I needed him in the worst way.

"Okay, tell me how." I smiled and stuck the gun back inside the table.

"Meet me at my sister's house," I said and disconnected the call.

I grabbed the end of the area run and tucked it tightly underneath Paris' body. I slowly rolled her in the rug and waited for Zane to arrive. Kadence came back into the living with a look of shock on her face.

"What did you do?"

"I eliminated the problem." I shrugged my shoulders and went out on the porch to wait for Zane.

18

KADENCE

Kenedee had lost her damn mind. I think Kyle had really gotten into her head.

"What did you do with the gun?" She pointed over to her shoulder to the table.

"Well, did you get any information before you got trigger happy with my baby upstairs?" I rolled my eyes.

"Nobody knows anything. You just go upstairs and tend to Kai; this will all be gone in the morning." I wanted to protest, but the movement in my stomach said otherwise.

"We're going to have to talk in the morning." Kenedee nodded her head and continued rolling that girl into the rug.

I didn't know what she had up her sleeve, but I would let her do her thing and step in if necessary. I walked up the stairs, trying to call Bryson again. The sun was already up, and I hadn't heard from him since he snuck out like a thief in the night. I had a doctor's appointment after I dropped Kai off at school, and I thought that he would be there. Bryson had been acting strange lately, and I prayed that it was just the hormones that had me feeling like he was acting suspicious. I went back in Kai's room and laid beside her. With everything that had been going on, I just wanted to keep her close. I wanted to know that she was safe like I had always promised her she would be.

WHEN I WOKE BACK UP, Bryson still was not home. I tried his cell again, and it was going straight to voicemail. I set out Kai's uniform and woke her up to get ready. I opened the door and called out to Kenedee, who didn't answer either. I went downstairs and just like she promised, the body and blood was gone like nothing ever happened. I called her phone, and she sent a text back that read.

Kenedee: Can't talk, I'm busy.

Me: Where are you?

Kenedee: Out with Zane. Be back later.

I made a mental note to get more information on Zane. Kenedee was being way too secretive, and that was not like her. I walked up to the master bedroom and pulled out a sweater and some jeans. While I was in the closet, I found a letter addressed to Bryson from State Farm. I hadn't noticed that he was having mail delivered to this address now, but I kind of liked it. It made things feel official and less whatever the hell they were. My curiosity got the best of me, and I wondered just what he was having sent here. I pulled the papers from the envelope and held them closely. It was a life insurance policy for half a million dollars, with me as the beneficiary. I was flattered that he thought enough of me to make me the beneficiary. At the same time, it made me wonder what the hell he was up to.

The Bryson that I had always known was a lame. He stayed at home, smoking and playing video games. This Bryson was unfamiliar. I don't ever remember a time when Jazelle complained of him not answering his phone. Now here I was looking like the bitch who couldn't take a hint. I stuck the paper back in the envelope and put it back where I had found it. I took a shower and got dressed. Kai was excited to get back to school. She had been out for a little over a month and today was her first day back. I wanted her to stay home. She missed her friends and teachers.

"Mommy, do you think Ms. Tate will remember me?"

"Of course she will."

"I sure hope so." She stared out the window. "Mommy?"

"Yes, Kai."

"Are you gonna be okay while I'm at school?" Kai was staring at me. Her face was serious.

"Yes, I am going to be just fine. I'm going to check on the baby and get some groceries, and then I'll be home waiting for you to get out of school." Kai looked skeptical.

"Maybe you should wait for Uncle B to do all of that." I smiled.

"Okay, if that's what you this is best." I wanted to put her mind at ease so that she could have a successful day at school. "You don't have to worry about mommy. I always come back." I smiled as I pulled into the circle drive in front of her school. "You want me to come in with you?" I started to unhook my seatbelt.

"No mom. Just be here after school. Don't be late." Kai jumped out of the car and ran over to a crowd of smiling, waving girls. I sat there until a car from behind me beeped their horn.

On my way to my doctor appointment, I tried Bryson again. This time he answered on the first ring.

"Good morning, beautiful."

"Don't beautiful me, nigga. Where are you?" There was a lot of noise in his background, but I couldn't make any of it out.

"I'm on my way home now."

"Did you forget we had an appointment today?" I pulled into a parking spot and turned off my car. I was a little early, but I was hoping my doctor would see me early. I made my way to the hospital entrance.

"No, I did not forget." Bryson stepped in front of me holding a smoothie and a single white rose. He smiled, but I still had an attitude.

"Sooooo, it's okay to stay out all night now? That's what we doing?" I snatched the cup from him. As irritated as I was, my mouth was watering for that strawberry smoothie. Bryson smiled and kissed my forehead.

"Hell naw that ain't what we doing, and I promise I won't let it happen again."

"So what was so important?" I put my hands on my hips and waited for an answer.

"Can we talk later? We do have somewhere to be."

Bryson put his hand on the small of my back and guided me through the door. I decided to let it go while we checked on our bundle of joy. Bryson sat across from me in the waiting room. Excitement was dripping from his face, but attitude was dripping from mine.

"So who were you with?"

"I told you Braylon needed my help."

"With what?" I fired back. Bryson shook his head and stared at me.

"I will tell you everything you want to know when we get home, but right here ain't the place, so just chill," Bryson said with so much bass in his voice that everyone in the room stopped talking.

I folded my arms across my chest and stared at him. The nurse called my name, and I followed her back to the exam room with Bryson on my heels. As soon as she got me settled in and closed the door, Bryson walked over to me at the table.

"I'm sorry. Please don't be mad." He weaved his fingers in between mine and kissed my hand.

"You said no lies! Keep it 100 at all times. Is that not what we agreed on?" Bryson took a deep breath.

"That is what we agreed and baby I swear I will tell you when the time is right. Just give me a little more time," Bryson pleaded with me, and I could no longer stay mad.

"Whatever." Bryson smiled and changed the subject.

"Have you talked to your mother today?" I shook my head. I hadn't realized until now that I had not, and that was weird. Mama usually called me as soon as her feet hit the floor.

"No, have you?" Bryson shook his head and kissed my hand again.

"Is she okay?" He nodded his head.

"She's fine. Just maybe we'll go see her after this." I ignored

Bryson and grabbed my phone from my purse. I dialed mama's number and got her voicemail too.

"Does anyone in this damn family know how to answer the damn phone?" I threw it back in my purse as the doctor walked in.

"Hello Kadence, how are we feeling today?"

"Annoyed." I rolled my eyes at Bryson. She went through the motions of checking my baby's heartbeat.

"Your blood pressure is unusually high. What's got you so bothered?"

"I'm fine." I brushed it off before her ass tried to admit me. The doctor squirted the cold gel on my belly and then used the Doppler, and the heartbeat filled the room.

"Heartbeat is good and strong. About 135 beats per minute." She measured the size of my abdomen and smiled. "We have you at about fifteen weeks. Sound about right?" I nodded my head and glanced at Bryson who was grinning from ear to ear.

"Is this your first child?"

"No, my second, his first." Bryson cleared his throat.

"When can we find out the sex?"

"Around 25 weeks, depending on how cooperative your baby is. "

"Knowing its mom, it will be stubborn," Bryson joked and smiled at me. Dr. Brooks smiled and handed me a tissue to wipe my belly.

"Is there anything you want to talk to me about?" I shook my head. She turned and looked at Bryson. "Any questions?" Bryson shook his head. "Okay. I'll see you in four weeks. Take care." She rushed out the room. Bryson helped me off the table.

"Did you eat?"

"Yes," I lied.

"I'm gonna get us some food and meet you at your moms." I rolled my eyes and grabbed my purse.

"Okay but I hope you have some answers when we get there."

I walked out the room and back to my car. I tried to call Jazelle, but her number was still disconnected. It was weird to me that she had just up and disappeared like that. After my talk with Bryson, I planned to find her. She had already proved to me that she could not be trusted. And, if it came down to me or her, it would most definitely be her.

19

BRYSON

I sat Kadence down on the bed and stared at her. She held a bag of nacho cheese Doritos in her lap. I focused on her stomach. She had my seed growing inside of her, and for that reason alone, my loyalty lied with her.

"I think Jazelle may be a problem."

"What kind of problem?" She stopped eating and looked at me with her beautiful grey eyes.

"One that needs to be handled." Kadence stopped fidgeting and stared at me.

"She's lost it, Kay and it's better you get her before she gets you. I met up with her yesterday." Kadence cut me off.

"That's where you were? With Jazelle?"

"Baby, don't lose focus on what I'm telling you. Jazelle is buggin', and she's coming after you first." Kadence stood up and started pacing the room.

"My sister?" she asked as if she was trying to make sure we were talking about the same person. "What do you mean get her?" I took a deep breath and grabbed both of her hands.

"Promise me you're not gonna go do some dumb shit when I say this." I paused. Kadence rolled her eyes and promised.

"I promise you I won't do nothin' stupid." She put a little more emphasis on the I than she should have, but I let it go.

"She's coked out. She's out here robbing people and running people over and shit."

"I knew she was weird last time I saw her, and that man she was fuckin' around with is a creep too. " I could see the wheels turning in her head.

"Remember what you promised me," I warned. Kadence waved me off and walked to the closet.

"I remember. Now explain to me why you were out all night."

I ran down the events of the night before from Bruce catching Zee lurking to Jazelle robbing Mama Lena and trying to kill Royce. Kadence jumped to her feet and ran to her mother's room.

"What the fuck, mama?"

"Watch your mouth."

"I'm sorry. Did Jazelle come here last night?" Mama Lena looked at me and then back at Kadence.

"Yes, she did."

"Alone?" Mama Lena dropped her head. Her voice got softer, her expression a little sadder.

"I didn't see anyone else." Kadence started pacing the floor. She rubbed her growing belly.

"So, what did she take?" Mama Lena looked up at Kadence and frowned.

"How did you know?"

"What did she take, mama?"

"Just some of the money I had saved up, nothing major." I stared at Mama Lena. Jazelle had told me how much she took. I couldn't understand why she was covering for her.

"How much money?" I asked. They both looked up at me.

$1,000 maybe."

"Mama! That is major! Why didn't you call me?"

"Because I know how you and Kenedee feel about her, and I don't want any more drama." Mama Lena stood in front of Kadence and cupped her chin. "Do you hear me?" Kadence snatched away and walked out of the room. Mama Lena looked over at me.

"What have you gotten yourself into?" She cracked a smile. I walked over and hugged her. She looked like she could use one. I reached into my pocket and handed her an envelope.

"Here, hang onto this for me." She opened it and looked inside.

"Bryson, there's over $2,000 in here!" she squealed as she flipped through the bills. "Why are you giving me this?"

"Just put it in your stash." Tears filled her eyes, and she pulled me into a hug. Mama Lena kissed me on both cheeks.

"You're a good man, Bryson. Just do me one favor?"

"Anything."

"Keep my girls out of trouble. I can't keep up with all the bullshit they get themselves into. Jazelle is playing a dangerous game, Kadence is emotional, and Kenedee is so damn unpredictable." She gripped her chest. "Jesus, protect my children."

"I promise to do my best. But in the meantime why don't you come back home with us?" Mama Lena shook her head and sat down on the bed.

"None of the coked out punks are going to run me away from my home."

"You need to be protected."

"I can hold my own." She looked at me with fire in her eyes. I pulled the Ruger from my pocket and handed it to her. I had given my mother one just like it for her birthday.

"What am I supposed to do with this, Bryson?" Mama Lena like looked up at me and smiled.

"Hold your own." I gave her another quick hug before walking over to the door. "One of us will be back later this evening." She nodded her head and examined the gun closely.

I walked up the hall to find Kadence sitting in her mother's chair.

"You good, babe?" I kneeled in front of her.

"Yeah, I'm good." She looked around the room avoiding eye contact with me, so I knew something was wrong.

"What's the problem?" Kadence fidgeted with her fingers and looked down at the carpet.

"It's just that you spent the night worrying about Jazelle like I wasn't at home waiting for you." I held her hands, partly because I wasn't sure how this would play out.

"I'm sorry. Jazelle called right when I pulled in the driveway. Had I known she was in Milwaukee when I agree, I would have never gone."

"Milwaukee? You left town for her?" I stood to my feet and let out a sigh I hadn't realized I'd been holding.

"Kadence baby, that's your sister. She called needing help."

"No. That's your ex. She needed help, but she didn't bother hittin' my line. She did, however, hit yours, and you went running. You made a fuckin' two-hour drive in the middle of the night to play captain save a hoe, without telling your girlfriend."

Kadence was shaking her finger and swiveling her neck in circles. Most niggas would have seen this as a sign to get out now, but me, I found that shit sexy. There was nothing sexier to me than knowing that your girl can go just as hard as you do.

"Baby, look at me." Kadence rolled her grey eyes in my direction. "I'm sorry I didn't tell you right away." I raised each of her hands and kissed them. "Please understand that what Jazelle and I had went out the window. She ain't the one for me, you are."

"You don't have any feelings for Jazelle? None whatsoever?" Kadence asked. Her eyes were sparkling. I knew she had something up her sleeve. I kissed he hands again.

"You are the one only girl in the world that I have feelings for— oh and Kai." A smile crept on her lips despite how hard she tried to fight it.

"I have a plan, but you gone have to roll with it. And it'll give you a chance to prove your loyalty to me."

"What's the word?" Kadence grabbed my hand and pulled me outside to the car. Once we were inside, she turned to me and smiled.

"I need you to fuck Jazelle."

I blinked my eyes and stared at her. I was sure I hadn't heard her right. Kadence popped open my glove compartment and handed me a blunt. I lit it and stared at her. I had heard of pregnancy making bitches crazy, but Kadence was in overdrive. "You think you can seduce her?"

She stared at me with wild eyes. I wondered if this was how she was when she came up with the plan to kill Loyal.

"I mean I haven't tried, but I probably could. Why?" Kadence squealed and clapped her hands together. I took a pull from my blunt and stared at her.

"I have the best plan, baby!"

"You're not gonna kill me are you?" She shook her head and laughed a little more loudly than I cared for.

My phone was vibrating, but I ignored it. I needed to see what Kadence was on first. I reached out and caressed her stomach. The baby in her stomach gave her a power over me that no person ever had before. I would do anything for Kadence, and it had been that way since day one.

"No. Well, not really."

"Not really? How the hell you not really kill someone?" Kadence walked over to the closet with one of the biggest smiles I had ever seen on her face.

"Okay, babe," she started, her eyes still sparkling. "This is what I think we should do." Kadence ran down her plan to me. I had to admit that shorty was a lot smarter than I initially thought she was.

"You think that'll work? Like really work? A nigga could go to jail for faking his death."

"As long as we do it right. Mistakes are what get you sent to jail," Kadence said.

Once again, I found myself wondering just how many people she had killed. Baby girl sounded like an expert, and I was almost positive that Loyal had not been her first.

Kadence positioned herself on my lap. "So whassup? You rockin' with me or not?"

"Always." She laughed and covered my mouth with hers. My dick immediately stood at attention. We kissed for a few seconds before I pushed her back to her side of the car.

"You don't wanna kiss me?" She frowned and started to get out of the car.

"I'm a grown ass man. I wanna do way more than kiss." I started the car and backed out of the driveway. Kadence giggled and slid her seatbelt on.

"You know I still want to know what went down with Braylon."

"I know, but as long as my seed is cooking. You gone wonder." She rolled her eyes and turned up the music, uninterested in anything else I had to say.

20

JAZELLE

My heart was beating fast. I paced the room and prayed that Bryson would not turn me in. When he came, I told him everything— from doing lines to robbing Mama Lena, to leaving Royce for dead in the middle of the road. I cried on his chest and apologized for everything I had done wrong to him in the past. He wiped my tears and told me everything would be fine, just like old times. He said he had to make some runs and that he would be back to get me and for some reason, I trusted him. I lit the blunt that he left with me. Somehow as soon as the smoke filled my lungs, I felt better. I don't know what I was thinking messing around with that other bullshit, but now I felt like I could see things clearly. I looked over at what was left of the money that I had taken from Mama Lena. I felt so bad. She was one of the few people who always had my back, and I had completely ruined that. I continued pacing. My stomach rumbled from lack of food. I opened the door to the shady motel room I was staying in. I looked up and down the street, but there was nothing that caught my attention. I was just about to order a pizza when a message popped up that damn near made my heart stop.

Royce: Where are you?

Feeling paranoid, I immediately turned my location off. I had run over Royce good. I couldn't understand how he was alive, let alone texting me. The phone buzzed again.

Royce: *Call me ASAP.*

I sat the phone on the bed and checked the locks on the doors and windows. Across the room, my phone continued to buzz. I couldn't look at it because I had no idea what to say. I leaned against the door and cried. Normally, in a situation like this, I would call Kadence. She would tell me exactly what to do and what to say to get a motherfucka off your ass. The phone finally stopped but was followed by a knock at the door.

"Open the door, Jazzy!" Kadence yelled from the other side of the door. I hurried and unlocked the door. I was ashamed to see her after all that I had done.

"Hey." I opened the door wide enough for her to step inside.

To say that Kadence looked stressed would be an understatement. She had huge bags under her eyes that she tried to hide with dark sunglasses. Her hair was usually laid, but now she covered it with a scarf that left a huge bow in the middle of her head.

"Hey. What's going on?" Kadence looked like she was on the verge of tears. She looked around the room and stared at me.

"Nothing you would want to hear about," she said as sat her purse down on the table.

"Tell me your troubles, and I'll tell you mine?" I asked as I handed her a Sprite from the mini fridge. Being around her so much, drinking them had become a habit of mine as well. Kadence sat down at the small table in the corner of the room and took a deep breath.

"Was Bryson with you all night?" She stared up at me.

"No. He came out this morning, but not all night. Why do you ask?" It was clear that Bryson had sold me out. But since I wasn't fighting for my life, I wasn't sure how much he had told her.

"He's been staying out all night. I swear it feels like when Loyal first started stepping out on me."

I stared at her. Kadence was absolutely right when she said it was something that I would not want to talk about. Hearing her cry about Bryson made me sick to my stomach.

"Bryson is nothing like Loyal," I defended him, and she looked at me sideways.

"That is true, but he's been acting really weird lately, and then I found this."

She pulled an envelope from her purse and handed it to me. A lump formed in my throat as I read the piece of paper. Half a mil for Kadence and her children if something happened to Bryson. If I didn't want to throw up before, I definitely did now. I wondered if he ever had that much trust in me. Kadence was rambling on about something, but I couldn't help but wonder what made Bryson choose her over me. She was basic to me; just another light skinned bitch with pretty eyes.

"So, what do you think?" Kadence stared at me with her eyes wide.

"I mean if that's what you want to do, sis. You know I'll ride for you regardless." I had no idea what she was talking about, but I spoke from the heart.

"So, you will help me kill Bryson?" I stared at her, trying to hide the shock I was feeling.

"Kill Bryson? I mean there has to be another way around it, right?"

"How else will we get the insurance money, Jazzy?" Kadence stood and slid her purse on her shoulder. My head was spinning. I would have never agreed to it had I known what she said.

"I don't know. Are you sure that's what you want? I mean you can't just kill every nigga who cheats on you. There is a word for people like that." She rolled her eyes.

"So, you're telling me, if you had the chance to get that type of money, you wouldn't take it?" I thought about it for a few seconds.

"I would, but look at what you would have to do to get it." Kadence put her hand on the doorknob, and then looked back at me.

"I know what you did to Royce and to my mama. You might want to stay on my good side before you become another one of the people on my list." Kadence smiled and walked out of the room.

My first instinct was to call Bryson and warn him about what Kadence was up to. My second thought was that he had just sold me out and proved that he wasn't really loyal to me. I knew that Kadence had lost her mind a long time ago so her threats could have very well been promises. I looked out the window in time to see Kadence walking into the office. I gathered my belongings and threw them into garbage liners from the hotel. I ran out to the car after making sure that I hadn't left anything behind and headed back to Madison. I didn't really have a plan, but I knew I needed more than what I had if I was going to be going up against Kadence.

I checked into a little motel right off the belt line under one of my aliases. This room was a step up from the one I had in Milwaukee, but not much. I picked up my phone and checked my Facebook something I hadn't done since this whole thing started. In damn near four months, I only had two unread messages. Not even the bored motherfuckas with no life cared to talk to me. I checked the messages, and there was one from Devon. I opened it, and it said three words.

Come see me.

All this time Devon had been trying to spend time with me, but I never considered the thought. Now, she was useful to what I needed. I pressed the icon to call her through Messenger. I was about to hang up, when she answered in a low tone.

"I don't do calls through Messenger; only creeps do that." I laughed.

"I didn't have your number, but I needed to talk to you." Devon perked up.

"I knew you wanted me, whassup baby?"

"I need to talk. Can you meet me somewhere?"

"Yeah, you okay?" It was nice to feel like someone cared for once.

"I will be. Can you come to Allied?"

"Allied? What the hell are you doing over there?"

"Slumming." I laughed. "I'll send you address," I said, but then I thought about it. "On second thought, send me yours."

"That's more like it. Are you bringing breakfast with you?" I looked in my bag and counted the bills I had left.

"Sure. What are you in the mood for?" Devon laughed.

"It's good, baby. Come through." Her voice was so smooth, and I started to wonder how many bitches she actually pulled. I grabbed my bag and keys and headed out the door. It was a short drive to where Devin was. She opened the door in a sports bra and some boxers.

"Whassup, Jazzy?" I stepped inside and gave her a quick hug.

"My whole world is falling apart." Devon led me over to a couch in the front room and sat beside me.

"What's going on?" I was skeptical about how much I could actually tell her.

"I need an alibi and somewhere to lay low." Devon laughed and lit the blunt lying in the ashtray.

"Y'all stay in some shit. Where's your sidekick?" she asked as she passed the blunt to me.

"Kicking it with somebody else I guess." I thought back to the night she had called Ashlee.

"Aww, poor baby. At least you knew where to come." She smiled. "So where have we been?"

"I've been here with you for the past two days."

"And where were you really?" she asked with a devilish grin on her face.

"Doing shit I couldn't have." My skin started to crawl. "I do need one more thing though."

"You know I got you."

"You know where I can get some coke?" Devon looked at me. Her face was almost sympathetic.

"Jazzy."

"I really don't need a lecture right now, Devon."

"But, you need my help, so you're gonna get one." She passed me the blunt and leaned closer to me. "That ain't you. Whatever got you hooked on that is over with. I'mma help you get off it." She got up and walked over to the kitchen counter. She opened a drawer and came back with a card.

"My brother is a counselor here. I'mma tell him you'll be there Monday." She handed the card to me. I looked it over.

"The Haven," I said the words quietly to myself. "Sounds corny."

"Yeah, well corny or not, you need it, motherfucka." I twirled the card between my fingers and hit the blunt again. It had been so long since smoking made me feel better.

"Maybe, I'll check it out."

"Ain't no maybe. You need an alibi, and I need you to get clean. Have your fun this weekend, because come next week, you're getting your shit together." Devon walked off again and returned with some towels. "The bathroom is up the hall on the right. The guest room is right across from that. My room is at the top of the stairs. You know if you get lonely."

"But, I paid for a room already."

"I'm sure mine is better." Devon winked at me as she walked up the stairs.

I walked around the house and was impressed by the way Devon lived. It was just her, and so far, I had counted three bedrooms already. Everything was white and gold, down to the tile that covered the floor. I turned on the light in the guest room. It was just as big as ever other room in the house. I took a shower and got comfortable in the bed. Tomorrow I would be ready for whatever came my way, but tonight I just wanted to sleep.

21

KENEDEE

I laid in the bed beside Zane. I didn't know what to make of his whole sister doing laundry thing, but I did know when I called he came. He loaded Paris' body in his van and helped me dump it in Lake Mendota, no questions asked. That was more than enough for me to overlook a bonnet and some lingerie that the bitch probably bought on Amazon.

"So, now what?" Zane asked, trying to catch his breath.

"Now, you make me that breakfast that you promised me." Zane smiled and kissed me on the forehead. "After all the work you just made me do? I'll take an omelet, please." I said trying to catch my breath after the way he had just put it down.

Zane fluffed his pillow and laid back on the bed. He folded his hands behind his head and looked at me. "What are you gone make yourself?" I snatched the pillow from beneath him and smacked his mouth across the face with it.

"I guess I'm having the same."

I grabbed a t-shirt from his drawer and walked out to the kitchen. I opened every cabinet until I found what I needed to make breakfast. I was almost done mixing the ingredients when I heard a key in the door. I stopped and stared at the door. I could hear Zane snoring in the other room, so he wouldn't be able to lie his way out of this one. The door opened, and a tall, dark skinned girl in a stewardess uniform walked in.

"Hello. Who are you?"

"I'm Ken. Who are you?" She pulled her suitcase into the kitchen and looked around.

"I'm Destiny. Are you making breakfast for everybody?" She kicked off her shoes and left me confused with a spatula in my hand. Not sure what to do, I followed her up the hall. She went in the room with Zane. I paused outside the door.

"Good morning, motherfucka!" Destiny yelled in Zane's ear. He jumped damn near falling out of the bed.

"Get out! Why are you here?" Zane moaned and rubbed his eyes.

"Who's the naked chick making eggs?" She picked up everything on his dresser and examined it before sitting it back down.

"None of your business and don't talk to her." Zane rolled from the bed and looked up at me standing in the doorway. "This is my little sister, the annoying one."

"Fuck you! I'm his favorite one. Why else would I have a key?"

"Because you stole it." She laughed and walked over and shook my hand.

"So, you're fuckin' my brother, huh? What's wrong with you?" Destiny laughed. She pushed my shoulder so hard that I damn near fell.

"Get out, Dee."

"Okay, okay. I just came to take a shower anyway. I'm off for the next week, and I'm on my way to see zaddy." Destiny stuck her tongue out and danced up the hallway. Zane walked over and kissed me.

"Are any of your sisters annoying like her?" I laughed.

"Actually, I am the annoying little sister." Zane smacked my ass, and I turned to finish making breakfast for everybody.

After we ate, I turned my phone on and checked my messages. There was one from Kadence telling me to come home ASAP.

"So, what do you have planned today, Ms. Kenedee?"

"I actually have to help my sister with something. What about you?"

"I have a few appointments this afternoon, but maybe I can link up with you later?" I nodded my head.

"We can definitely make that happen." I fought the urge to smile. Destiny came back through the apartment looking like a completely different person. Her long dark hair was now short and purple. She danced in front of the full-length mirror in the living room.

"Bald head baddie, steal yo' baby daddy." She giggled to herself before turning to me. "Nice to meet you, Ken. Hope to see you again soon. I'll be back to get my stuff, big head." She smacked Zane upside his head on her way out.

"And that's how you found her shit in the bathroom." I got up and cleared the dishes from the table. Zane walked up behind me and wrapped his arms around me.

"Can I ask you one question?"

"Of course." I turned around to face him.

"Exactly how many people have you killed?" The question caught me by surprise, but I could see why he was wondering.

"What makes you think I killed her?"

"Why else would you need help hiding the body and re-tiling the floors?" I pulled him close and kissed him. I hoped that it would buy me some time to come up with an answer that didn't sound like straight bullshit.

"Is it a problem for you?"

"A problem that you kill people, or a problem that you don't want to tell me how many people you've killed?"

"Both." Zane smiled showing off his deep dimples.

"Naw, I actually think it's kind of sexy. You're like a secret weapon." I burst out laughing.

"How?" He pushed me up against the refrigerator. I jumped up and wrapped my legs around him.

"That's why. You look so sweet and innocent, but then it's like surprise! I'm a gangsta in real life."

We both started laughing. Zane kissed my neck and unbuttoned my shirt. Kadence's ringtone filled the room. I tried to ignore her, but she kept calling. Zane let me down, and I grabbed my phone from the counter.

"Hey, Kay."

"Hey, Ken." I leaned over the marble island. Zane still behind took the opportunity to remove my pants and underwear. I looked over my shoulder, but he had disappeared.

"Some shit went down, and I think you need to know." I could tell by the tone in her voice that it was serious.

"Is mama okay?"

"Yeah, she's fine. Are you still with the carpet cleaner?" I rolled my eyes and went to find my clothes.

"His name is Zane, and yes I am." Zane was lying in the bed. I saw my pants sticking out from under his pillow. When I reached for them, he grabbed my arm and pulled me into the bed.

"Kay, I'll meet you in an hour." I leaned in and kissed Zane. "And a half." I hung up the phone and dropped it to the floor. Zane and I made love for the third time since we had woken up that morning.

"Can I ask you a question?" I propped myself up on my elbows and stared at him.

"What's on your mind?"

"Have you ever killed anyone?" Zane closed his eyes for a minute.

"I have before. Is that a part problem for you?" I shook my head and stood to walk towards the bathroom.

"Actually, I think it's kind of sexy." I laughed and took a quick shower before meeting Kadence.

Ever since she got pregnant, it didn't take much to get her worked up. So, this meeting she wanted was probably something as small as me not bringing back the Doritos she asked me to get. When I came out, Zane was dressed and standing in the living room. He had his back turned to me, but I could hear that he was on the phone.

"No, sir. We're right on schedule. I'll check back with you Monday."

"I thought you were your own boss." I said as I snuck up behind him. Zane turned around and kissed me.

"I am. That was just a customer. You need a ride home?" I nodded my head, and I slipped my feet in my sandals.

"Yes. I have to start driving my own car." Zane laughed and held the door open for me.

"You don't have to. I like driving you around."

"Why so you can keep tabs on me?"

"Exactly." Zane flashed that smile again. Each time he did, I felt butterflies in my stomach. I had Zane drop me off at mama's house. Even though it was unusually cold for that time of year, mama was sitting on the porch with her Kindle in her hand.

"Hey mama, what you reading?"

"*Trapped By This Thing Called Love* by T. Smith. You ever heard of her?" I shook my head and sat down beside her.

"Naw, is she new?"

"Yeah, another Mz. Lady P author; you know they're always writing good shit." I laughed. Mama read more urban fiction than anybody I knew. Every time we watched a movie and asked her opinion, her response was always the same. "It was good, but I bet the book was better."

"I found another book you might like mama, *No Way Out* by Latoya Nicole. Have you heard of her?" Mama nodded her head with a huge smile on her face.

"Yes! Did you know that it was based on a true story? Girlllll." Mama stretched that word out way longer than it should have been. "And what the hell is gay for the stay?" I burst out laughing.

"Nothing you need to worry about. You okay out here alone?" Mama looked at me over the top of her glasses.

"I was alone before you came, wasn't I?"

"You're right. Is Kadence inside?" Mama was already laughing at her book. She didn't even realize I had walked away. I walked through the house and noticed that no one was there. I pulled my phone out of my purse and called Kadence. She answered on the first ring, out of breath.

"Hey, Ken."

"Hey, Kay. Where are you?"

"I'm home." She moaned loudly. I held the phone away from my ear.

"You are so disgusting!"

"I'm on my way. Aw, shit! Baby, I'm coming!" she yelled before the line went dead.

"Ewww! She always does that shit!" I got my iPad and joined mama on the porch.

"What's been going on since I've been gone, mama?" I got comfortable in the big wicker chair across from her.

"Nothing much, the regular," she said without looking up from her Kindle.

"Mama, can I ask you a question?" She took a deep breath and looked up at me.

"What, Kenedee?" I picked at a loose string on my jeans, trying to avoid the death stare she was giving me.

"What's the real reason you hid the truth about Jazelle for so long?" I finally looked at her. Her anger was replaced with sadness.

"I don't know. I didn't want to face the fact that I had turned my back on one of my children. That's why I go so hard about you being there for one another. I may not be around too much longer."

"Mama, you always say that! You're too stubborn to go anywhere." She smiled, but the pain was still in her eyes.

"I mean it, Kenedee."

"I know, mama. I'll try to be nicer, but I know she grimy as fu- I mean super grimy. Just look at what she's done so far." Mama wiped the tears that had begun to fall. I got up and wrapped her in a hug.

"I didn't mean to make you cry." Mama patted my arm and eased up from her chair.

"Jazelle needs this family. We need to be there for her, end of story."

She turned and walked in the house. I followed her inside and went to her room. Mama always kept important letters in a box, on her dresser. I shuffled through the envelopes until I found the one from the adoption agency and stuck it in my purse.

"Tell Kadence I'll be right back, mama." I got in my car and drove to the agency. It was far from what I expected. The office was gloomy. The walls were dark, years of handprints and memories left by the children who played there.

"Good morning. What can I do for you?" I smiled and pulled the envelope from my bag.

"Morning, I need to speak to whoever mailed this letter." I handed it to her and all of the color drained from her face.

"That would be me, ma'am. How can I help you?" All of a sudden, she was more professional.

"I think there was a mistake. Maybe your records got mixed up or something. Jazelle isn't my sister." I leaned forward and placed my hand on her desk.

"Well, how do you know?"

"DNA don't lie." I stared at her. She looked at the man sitting beside her. He looked back and forth between the two of us like he was watching his favorite sitcom glued to the edge of his seat.

"Maybe we should go to my office?" She stood and walked around the desk.

"Naw, we can talk here." I folded my arms across my chest. The woman turned her back to the desk and whispered to me.

"Okay, look, Jazelle came in here and donated a lot of money for that paper— something that we obviously need around here. These kids need help." I held my hand up to stop her.

"Save the speech. Where's the real paperwork? And I don't wanna hear none of that it's against the rules bullshit because you obviously do what you want." She rolled her eyes and stormed into her office. She came back with a huge folder.

"This is Jazelle's file. Your real sister died some time ago. Her death certificate is in there as well. Tell Jazelle don't bring her crazy ass back in here either." She walked over to the door and held it open for me. I smiled and slid my sunglasses on. I handed her five one hundred dollar bills.

"Thanks! You have a great day!" I absolutely could not wait to spill this tea. I sped back to the house, thinking of ways to expose Jazelle for the fraud that she was.

22

KADENCE

I took a shower and headed over to mama's house after picking Kai up from school. Mama and Kenedee were sitting in the living room; mama was asleep in her chair as usual. Ken was watching *Steve Harvey*.

"Hey, Ken."

"Hey, Kay. What y'all up to?"

"I need to talk to you and mama." Kenedee put down the remote and followed me into the back of the house. She had been quiet since our run-in with Paris. The only time she smiled was when Zane was involved. I figured it was time to come clean and fill Kenedee in on my plan. There wasn't a doubt in my mind that this one would definitely make her feel better. Kai took her usual place in front of the TV, while Kenedee and I walked up the hall to mama's room. I knocked on the door. My mind was already racing on ways to end this shit once and for all. Bryson had spent so much time convincing me he was the good guy, but now I needed to see his bad side. He assured me before I left the house that everything would work out fine as long as I remembered to stick to the plan as if I ever had any problem in that area.

"Come in." I opened the door and waited for Kenedee to close the door before I started spilling the tea. As soon as she closed it, there was a knock on the door.

"Hey, mama." I wrapped her in a hug. Okay, so I'm about to unload a lot on y'all at once. I'm so sorry for everything." Mama sat down in the bed and turned on the small lamp that sat on her bedside table.

"Are the kids okay?"

"Yes, my kids are fine. Yours, on the other hand, not so much." Kenedee sat at the foot of the bed and stared at me.

"I don't really know where to start. So I guess I'll go back to Loyal." I rubbed my hands together. Somehow, I felt like confessing to my mama was like having to face God one on one and tell him about your sins.

"A few months ago, Jazelle and I talked about killing Loyal. I never really thought I would go through with it until the motherfucka shot me. I only had amnesia for a couple of days, the rest of the time I was faking it to keep up with my cover. Before I left the hospital, I texted Jazzy and told her to bail Loyal out. Then I had Bryson take me back to the house, where I killed Loyal before Ken had the cleaners come."

I paused and looked at Kenedee who looked like a lightbulb had just gone off in her head. I sat down on the bed next to her. She reached out and grabbed my hand.

"It was pure luck that Kenedee wasn't there when we were. To be completely honest I don't know how she wasn't there. But anyway, we hid the body in Jazelle's car and took it to be disposed of."

"Kadence, what the hell is going on?" Mama clutched her imaginary pearls. I took a deep breath and continued my story.

"A few weeks ago, I found a life insurance policy for Bryson with me listed as the beneficiary, so I came up with another plan to get his money as well." I swallowed hard, suddenly feeling like a monster. "Jazelle has changed. She ain't rocking with us no more. She needs to be treated accordingly." For the first time for as long as I can remember, both my mother and my little sister were speechless. Kenedee was the first to speak.

"So, what's the plan now?" I shrugged my shoulders. I didn't really know what to do at this point. Everything I had planned was falling apart. Mama stood and walked over to her dresser.

"I got a new plan." She spoke up as she pulled an envelope from her top drawer. She handed it to me and squeezed between the two of us. I opened the envelope, and there was a deed to a house in Texas.

"What is this mama?" She reached for both of our hands.

"This is a house that I purchased. I knew that things would get worse before they got better, so I planned ahead. It's about an hour from Mexico. You think maybe it's time we moved?" She looked at me with a hopeful look on her face. I read over the papers, and everything seemed legit.

"Mama, how the hell did you buy a house without me knowing? I have been paying your bills for years!" She smiled and pulled a suitcase from her closet.

"Loyal has been paying, and that gave me extra money to make moves with." Kenedee still hadn't said much.

"What you think, Ken? Are you up for a change of scenery?" Kenedee nodded her head and walked out of the room.

"What's her problem?" Mama shrugged her shoulders and continued to sort through her clothes. Once we agreed to the move, everything else I had said before was gone from her mind. "I'm going to go check on her." I followed Kenedee and met her outside of the bathroom door.

"Ken, you okay?" I knocked lightly on the door. She opened it with her face flushed and her eyes watering.

"I'm fine. My stomach just hurts." I put my hand on her shoulder.

"I'm sorry I left you out."

"It's okay, just count me in this time." I frowned my face confused.

"This time? Didn't you hear what mama just said?"

"Yeah. I heard her say we were leaving the country. I also heard you say that Jazelle crossed the line again. So, my question to you is, how do you want to take her out?" I chuckled until I realized that Kenedee was not.

"She is still our sister, Kenedee." Kenedee pulled me into the spare bedroom that she had taken over and handed me a birth certificate.

"I found this a few days ago. I was just waiting on the right time to bring it up." I looked over what appeared to be Jazelle's birth certificate.

"Kenedee, this is probably from her adoptive parents." I tried to hand her the paper back, but she pushed another one towards me.

"Uh huh, then what is this?" It was another birth certificate similar to the one I held in my hand, only the seal of approval was missing from one. The one that had my mother's name on it was fake and had the date had also been altered.

"Where did you find this, Kenedee?"

"When I found the right one, I went to the adoption agency and pretended to be Jazelle and had them fax a copy of the one they had on file. The lady Mackenzie that was over the case said that for some reason there were two certificates and she would have to investigate. Long story short, Jazelle is not our fuckin' sister. This birth certificate is a fake and Jazelle's ass deserves whatever is coming to her." I stared at the papers trying to find something that would make Kenedee a liar, but there was nothing. "So, I'll ask you again, how do you want to take her out? I folded the papers and handed them back to Kenedee.

"Meet me at my house later tonight. I need to figure this shit out."

I walked back into the living room and sat down on the couch next to Kai. I pulled out my phone. I had copied her new number from Bryson's phone. I hesitated before I sent a text to Jazelle. I didn't understand how things had gotten so bad so fast.

Me: What's good?

Kai laid her head in my lap.

Jazelle: We need to talk.

I ignored her message and wrecked my brain. I knew Jazelle had been on drugs lately, so there was really no telling where her head was. I really didn't understand what she could gain by pretending to be related to us, but I planned on finding out.

Me: Meet me at mama's.

I waited for her to lie and tell me she was out of town. Devon had already called last night and told me she was sleeping in her guest room.

Jazelle: Okay, gimme a minute.

I leaned back and waited for her to arrive, operation get rid of Jazelle was in effect.

About 30 minutes later, Jazelle walked through the door. Her dreads were tucked under a baseball cap. She wore no makeup, and her clothes were dirty.

"Hey family," she whispered as she walked inside. She went to hug mama, but she got up and walked from the room. Always being the observant one, Kenedee stood to follow mama.

"What was that about, Jazzy?" Jazelle shrugged her shoulders and plopped down on the sectional next to Kai.

"Hey, TT baby! How you been?"

"I've been good, TT. Where you been?" Jazelle looked at me and then back at Kai.

"I had a lot of things I had to get in order, but I'm better now. We need a girl's day. What do you think?" Kai nodded her head with a huge smile on her face.

"Jazelle; can I talk to you outside for a minute?" Jazelle finally removed her glasses and stared at me.

"Sure Kay." She followed me outside on the porch.

"Have you given any thought to what I asked you?" Jazelle pulled a cigarette from her bag and lit it.

"Yeah, I thought about it. What's the plan?" I smiled.

"Good. Just wait for my text. When you get it, meet me at the house. The less you know the better."

I turned and walked back inside the house. I sent a text to Bryson that everything was on schedule. Jazelle had no idea what was in store for her.

23

JAZELLE

I sat on the porch and checked my voicemails from my old phone. Many were from Royce, but there was one that caught my attention.

"*Jazelle, its Mackenzie. Your sister has been snooping and asking a lot of questions. She knows the paperwork isn't authentic. Call me back.*" At that moment I felt like my heart would stop. There was no way either of them had that type of information and was just sitting on it. I played the message again to make sure I had heard her correctly.

"Aw Fuck!" I yelled and started pacing the porch. I thought back to when I first met Mackenzie.

"GOOD MORNING! *How may I help you?*" Mackenzie asked way too happy for the time of day. I looked around the adoption agency that had definitely seen better days.

"*What type of funding do you all get?*" Mackenzie rolled her eyes.

"*Whatever donations are made they are from the community.*"

"*What if I could give you $10,000?*" Her eyes lit up. Mackenzie poured me a cup of coffee and escorted me to her office.

"I'm sorry I didn't catch your name." She extended her hand towards me.

"I'm Jazelle; I grew up in a place like this. I'm always looking for ways to give back."

"That's awesome! I can get you a receipt to get a tax credit as well."

"Actually, I need something from you as well." I paused while I tried to find the words. "I'm trying to find my birth mother. Well, I've already found her; I just want to make things official." The smile disappeared from her face.

"I'm not sure I follow you." Mackenzie shifted uncomfortably in her seat.

"I was an orphan. I found the lady I want to make my birth mother, and I'm willing to give you, I mean your organization, $10,000 to make that happen for me. All I need is a birth certificate. I can handle the rest."

"All you need?" Mackenzie chuckled. I pulled the envelope containing $15,000 inside.

"I can see you're conflicted. Maybe an extra five for you would help." Mackenzie stood and walked around the desk.

"I'm sorry, ma'am. That's not the way we do things here." She walked over to the door and opened it. I walked over to the door and closed it. I put the envelope in her empty hand and put my Beretta to her head.

"I don't think you understand, Mackenzie. You don't really have much choice in the matter. And, after everything is done, I need you to call this number and ask for Kalena Jones. Inform her that her birth daughter has been found." I waited for Mackenzie to respond. She slowly nodded her head.

"Okay, it will take a few days. If you leave your number, I can call you when everything is done," Mackenzie reassured me, with tears in her eyes.

"Thanks a bunch, Kenz!" I tucked my baby back in my purse. "Oh, and Mackenzie?" She had run over to her desk and was leaning over the edge of it, holding her chest.

"Yeah?" Her voice held so much attitude.

"You don't want me to come back here, right?"

"No, I don't."

"Glad we're on the same page." I walked out of the office, slamming the door behind me.

I WAS on my way to my car when Kai ran outside.

"You're leaving already, TT Jazzy?" I turned and went back to hug her.

"Yeah, sweetheart; I'll be back soon though. Be good for your mommy, keep her out of trouble okay?" Kai nodded her head.

"You promise?" She stared up at me with her huge brown eyes. She was the spitting image of her father.

"Yeah, baby girl. I promise." I kissed her on her forehead and ran to the car. I knew if I didn't do anything else. I had to warn Bryson that his life was in danger. I drove back to Devon's to collect my thoughts.

Devon greeted me at the door with an extendo blunt. I knew that she had ratted me out to Kadence, but there was a lot of that going on, so I couldn't hold it against her.

"Hey, Dev. How was your day?" I took the blunt from her and lit it.

"Any day above ground is a good one to me," she said and picked the remote up from the coffee table and turned on the TV. "So listen, I've been thinking." Devon paused and turned to face me.

"I'll be gone tonight," I said before she even got the chance.

"I wasn't going to kick you out, Jazelle. I just wanted to make sure you would be there, Monday. My brother is expecting you."

"I can quit without rehab." Devon frowned and turned off the TV.

"That's what all addicts say." I passed her the blunt and walked towards the guest room.

"Let's not act like you're really concerned. We both know you could give two fucks."

"I'm not who you should be mad at."

"Yeah? Well, you're not somebody I should fuck with either." I grabbed my bag and met Devon at the door.

"Jazelle, I really don't think this is gonna end well for you." She stood in front of me with her hands on her hips. Her usual calm demeanor was gone. She was clearly annoyed, and I could care less. Everybody thought they knew what was best for me but were turning their backs on me at the same time.

"I can hold my own." I walked out the door and got in my car. Kadence texted me, as soon as I put the key in the ignition.

Kadence: I'm home.

I sat the phone in the passenger seat and drove to Kadence's house. The whole way there, I tried to think of a way to get Kadence to change her mind. I came up on a lick that we could really hit that would make both of us set and keep Bryson alive. A small part of me still loved that man. Loyal, I could do without. It was never love between us. It had always been straight fuckin'. No matter how many times we swore we would never do it again, somehow he always ended up between my legs.

I pulled into the driveway behind Kadence's car. When I got out, she was on the porch.

"Hey."

"Hey, I need you to go to the hospital and pick this stuff up from Mya tomorrow. I'm gonna put it in his drink, and he will die in his sleep. Just act like you're coming over to visit and leave it in the vase in the kitchen. Okay?" I nodded my head because I couldn't get the words to come out. I couldn't get any words to come out. I felt numb.

"You okay, Jazzy? You don't look so good." Again, unable to speak, I nodded my head.

Kadence waited a few seconds before turning and going back in the house. She left me standing on the porch, nodding my head like a damn fool. I walked back to my car and pulled off. It was time to pay Mackenzie a visit.

I pulled up in front of her house. I knew that she was home because the bitch didn't have a life outside of those damned kids. I tucked my gun inside my hoodie pocket and walked up to her door. It was dark outside, and the rain had made the temperature drop. I rang the doorbell and waited. I could see through the glass door that Mackenzie was sitting alone on the couch watching TV. I rang the doorbell again, and she slowly got up and walked to the door.

"Jazelle? What are you doing here?" I pushed my way inside and turned to face her.

"You didn't hold up your part of the deal, Mackenzie. I thought you said we had an understanding." The color drained from her face, and she looked around the room.

"What are you looking for? You tryin' to hit me or something?" I asked, smiling and walking closer to her.

"She was going to go to the police. My whole organization would have been shut down. I couldn't let that happen." Her usually perky voice was low and fearful.

"But you took my money though?" I stared at her. "So, you can either give that back, right now or..." I pulled the pistol from my pocket. "It's your choice, though" I shrugged my shoulders and smiled. Mackenzie started to cry, which told me which option she chose. "You really fucked me over, Mackenzie." I cocked the pistol and pointed it at her stomach.

"Jazelle, please I can fix this."

"How?" I paused to see what she could come up with. I didn't want to hurt Mackenzie, but she had me fucked up. She continued to look around the room until her eyes focused on a hammer sitting on the table next to me. I followed her stare and laughed.

"Really? A hammer, Mackenzie." I walked over and smacked her in the head with the butt of the gun. "Bitch, I have a fuckin' gun! What the hell is wrong with you?" Mackenzie cried out in pain and stared at me.

"Jazelle, I'm sorry."

"Sorry didn't do this, you did. Did you have my money or naw?" I chuckled. Her eyes grew wide, and she struggled to find the words.

"I-I- can have it..." I pulled the trigger. One shot to the head, one to the chest." I stepped over her body and walked back to my car.

I had another plan to save Bryson. I guess you could call it a last resort. I stopped at Woodman's and got something to keep my stomach from rumbling. Forgetting about Mackenzie's blood, I walked through the produce section, looking for something to eat.

"Ma'am, are you alright?" I turned and looked at the short Asian man who was sitting in the middle of the floor surrounded by boxes of fruit.

"Yeah, thanks for asking."

I grabbed some apples, a loaf of bread, some turkey, and a two-liter of Sprite and paid for the items. Everyone stared, but to my surprise, no one said anything. I walked back to my car. I drove back to across town in silence. I stopped a little up the block, parked on the other side of the street so that I had a clear view of Kadence's house. I pulled the blanket I had taken from Devon's house from the backseat and covered myself.

I HEARD KAI'S VOICE, and it woke me from my sleep.

"Have a good day, Uncle B. See you later."

I sat up in the seat just in time to see her and Kadence getting into the car. I reclined the seat and waited for them to go past. Bryson was standing on the porch with no shirt. My pussy instantly started throbbing. Once Kadence was gone, I pulled up in front of the house. I got out and used my key to let myself in. I stopped in the foyer and popped one of my anxiety pills. I walked through the house and remembered all of the good memories that I had there. Surprisingly, they still outweighed the bad. I walked up the stairs in search of Bryson. When I got to the top of the stairs, I could hear the shower running. I went inside the master bedroom and waited on the bed. I still didn't know what I was going to say; I just knew that we needed to talk, fast. Bryson walked out the bathroom completely naked. I gasped at the sight of his dick swinging.

"What the fuck you doing here, Jazelle?" He pulled a bath towel from the door and wrapped it around his glistening body.

"I uh, I needed to talk to you."

"Can it wait until I'm not naked?" Bryson opened the door and waited beside it.

"Bryson, I've seen you naked plenty of fuckin' times. That is the least of your worries right now." I closed the door and snatched his towel off. I couldn't keep my eyes off of his dick. It wasn't even fully hard, and it laid against leg like a baby anaconda.

"Jazelle! Get out!" Bryson did all that yelling, but he still didn't move me which we both knew he could.

I dropped to my knees and took him in my mouth. Bryson grabbed my dreads, but I just slid more of him in my mouth. He had to miss the way I used to do him. There was no way Kadence could suck and fuck him the way that I could. I mean there was a reason Loyal never left me alone. I spit on his dick and went to work just the way he liked it. Bryson's knees buckled.

"Jazelle, move!" Bryson snatched my hair again, but I just sucked harder.

It was cute, the way he was pretending to be a faithful ass, good guy type of nigga. Bryson was not the man that he wanted everybody to think he was. Bryson moaned, and I knew I had him right where I wanted him. I got up and pulled him over to the bed. I mean, I felt like it was only right that I fucked him where she laid her head. I pushed him down and went back to it. I was trying to suck the skin off that nigga dick so that he knew which one of us he should really be with. Bryson's dick was rock hard, so I stopped sucking and jumped on top of him. I rode Bryson and smiled. Everybody hates me for doing the things that I do, except these niggas. If you loved me before, you would always love me. Bryson dug his nails into my hips as he drilled me. I came hard all over his dick and dove under the covers to lick it off. Bryson moaned and pushed my head down, making his dick going further down my throat.

"Aw fuck!" he moaned, and I could tell he was about to come.

I snaked my tongue around his dick as he massaged my neck. I laid flat on my stomach and sucked his balls while jacking him off. Bryson's body stiffened when I slowly slid my mouth down the length of his dick. He came in my mouth just as I heard a voice ask.

"What the fuck?"

24

KENEDEE

I laid across the bed and thought about what mama had just said. Moving to Texas wasn't my first choice, but neither was staying in Wisconsin. My mama and my sister were all that I had, and nobody mattered more to me. I wasn't sure I could even make it without them. I rolled over and stared at my phone. As if he could read my mind, Zane's picture popped up, and my phone began to vibrate.

"Hey, how are you?" I couldn't fight the smile that was forming on my lips.

"Hey beautiful, are you busy tonight?"

"I might be, why? What do you have planned?" I was already up and looking through my closet for something to wear.

"I wanna take you out for dinner. I have something I need to talk to you about."

"Okay, what time should I be ready?"

"I'll pick you up at seven o'clock."

I pulled a white maxi dress from the closet and held it to my body in front of the mirror. I laid the dress across the bed and tossed the many different white shoes that I had acquired over the years from the closet.

"I could drive my own car."

"It wouldn't be a date if I didn't pick you up," Zane said. I could tell from the way he spoke that he was smiling too.

"Okay, whatever you say. I'll be ready."

I went and took a shower and wash my hair. I tried on the dress and changed my mind. It wasn't tight enough. Two hours, twelve dresses and fifteen pairs of shoes later, I admired myself in the mirror. The all white Gucci jumpsuit hugged my body in all the right places. The crystals along the hem sparkled when the light hit them. I smiled as I turned around and adjusted the straps. I grabbed the diamond earrings and necklace that Kyle had given me on our first date and put them on. I decided on a pair of Christian Louboutin heels and pulled my hair into a tight bun.

"You look real fancy!" mama exclaimed when I walked in the living room with a little over 30 minutes to spare.

"Thank you! I have a hot date."

"With the carpet man?" Mama stared at me with her mouth wide open.

"He owns it, and yes with Zane."

"Well, look who finally realized money isn't everything." I sat down on the couch beside her and smiled.

"You're right, mama. It isn't." A few minutes later Kadence walked in with Kai on her heels.

"Hey y'all. Where are you going?"

"Out with Zane." I couldn't stop smiling, just saying his name. Kadence smiled and sat across from us. Kai grabbed the remote and turned to the Disney channel.

"Can I stay here tonight, Grammy?"

"Of course you can." Kai loved to stay with mama because she could do whatever she wanted. Kadence had rules, but mama didn't.

I pulled out my phone to check the time, and the doorbell rang. I got up to answer the door. Zane stood there wearing a three-piece suit and that smile that drove me crazy.

"Hey, gorgeous."

"Hey, babe." I jumped in his arms and kissed him, forgetting my family was watching. Mama, on the other hand, didn't miss a beat.

"Hello, I'm Kenedee's mother." Zane kissed her hand and handed her a bouquet of roses he had been hiding behind his back.

"Nice to meet you, ma'am." Mama smiled and took the roses.

"Oohhh, I like this one, Ken!" She took off down the hall towards the kitchen to put them in water. Kadence stood to her feet, her small pudge poking from underneath her shirt.

"Hey Zane, how are you?" Zane shook hands with Kadence and smiled.

"I'm very well, thanks for asking." Zane turned to me and linked his arm in mine. "Are you ready to go?" I nodded my head and followed him out the door. Zane had changed from the usual company van that he drove and had a dark colored Lincoln LS parked out front.

"Who's car is this?" I asked as he opened my door and helped me into the car.

"My sister." He closed the door and jogged to the other side. "You look beautiful, by the way." I was glad the darkness could hide my smile. I just knew my face was bright red from blushing.

"So where are we going?"

"L'Etoile. You ever been?" I shook my head and grabbed his hand.

I silently prayed that Zane was not married, and I would not have to kill him. Zane talked about the jobs that he had done, and I was actually interested. We pulled into the parking lot, and I waited for Zane to open my door. We linked arms and Zane marched through the restaurant like he owned the place until we reached the table in the center of the room. Everyone in the room was watching as we took out seats, and I loved it! The waiter came to the table before my ass even hit the chair.

"Good evening, may I start you with some drinks?" he said in a French accent that was so horrible; I probably could have done better.

"We'll have a bottle of your best red wine." Zane winked at me, and I was still beaming. When the waiter was gone, Zane reached for my hand across the table.

"I have something I need to talk to you about. Would you rather do it here or at home?" I felt butterflies in my stomach when he said home. I had never been the wifey type, but for Zane, I might have played the role.

"Let's enjoy our dinner first. We have all night, right?" Zane smiled and kissed my hand.

"Okay. I have something for you, but you'll have to wait for that too." Zane smiled and dropped my hand.

"You tricked me!" I pouted.

The waiter came back with our drinks and took our dinner order. Zane and I had the perfect dinner, in public. It felt nice not having to hide from anyone. I excused myself to the ladies room, while Zane settled the check. When I came out, he was waiting for me by the front door. I couldn't keep my hands off of him as he drove across town to his apartment.

"Kenedee, you're gone make me crash."

"Or make you drive faster. A little over the speed limit never hurt nobody." Zane smiled and kissed me. I felt the car jerk as he accelerated. From the car to the front door we were all over each other.

"As bad as I want to make love to you baby, we need to talk."

"Okay, I'm listening." I flicked my tongue in his ear and massaged his dick through his pants.

"Um, I need to tell you something."

"Uh-huh, you said that already." I kissed his neck and unbuckled his belt.

"I don't really own a flooring business," He said. His breathing had started to pick up. There was no denying the bulge in his pants meant that he was just as ready to fuck as I was. I eased his dick out and into my mouth. Zane leaned back on the couch and moaned loudly.

"Fuck, Ken!" he yelled, and I took more and more of him into my mouth. "I'm undercover." I stopped and looked up at him. My heart leaped into my throat as we locked eyes.

"Undercover what?"

"An undercover officer. I'm officer Zane Michaels, Madison PD." My mind was flooded with thoughts of everything that I was dumb enough to involve him in over the past few weeks. I jumped up and backed away from him.

"You're the police? Oh my god! You're the fucking police?" I paced the floor, with my head in my hands and tried to figure out how I could have been so stupid.

"Kenedee, relax." Zane tried to hug me, but I jumped away from him.

"Relax? How? I'm going to jail!" I cried. "I'm so fucking stupid! I thought you actually liked me!" Tears fell from my eyes. Zane watched me panic for a few seconds before walking over to his pants that were lying in the middle of the floor.

"Kenedee, please relax. You are not going to jail." I stopped pacing and stared at him.

"What about my sisters?" He held out his hand and pulled me close to him.

"We were investigating Jazelle Green. I thought that maybe you could help me arrest her for the murder of Loyal Jackson."

"Loyal? You're working his fucking case?" I snatched my hand away again and picked up my shoes.

"If I'm not under arrest, that means I can leave, right?" Zane snatched my shoes and threw them on top of the refrigerator.

"Listen to me, damn it!" Zane yelled and grabbed both of my hands.

"The more time I spent with you, the more I fell in love. I could never put you in a place like that, so I have a plan."

"A plan?" I stared at him like he had lost his mind. Zane opened a small black box that held the biggest fuckin' diamond I had ever seen. Zane got down on one knee and smiled.

"Kenedee Jones, will you marry me?" I looked around the room, almost certain that Ashton Kutcher would pop out at any second and tell me I was being punked.

"Is this a joke?"

"No, it's not a joke." I looked at the ring. Even in the dark, that motherfucka was shining.

"Why would we get married, Zane?" Zane slid the ring on my finger.

"I can't testify against my wife. That makes everything that you've told me and everything that I helped you with, nonexistent in my eyes." He paused and looked up at me. "If you say yes." It was really a no-brainer. I smiled at the ring that weighed down my finger.

"Of course I'll marry you!"

Zane pulled me into a bear hug and swept me off my feet. We kissed, and he carried me to the bedroom. We made love that night like we never made love before. I couldn't wait to become Zane's wife. It was a major step up from what I had been doing. I'll soon be police officer's wife— a crooked one at that. It sounded like the perfect set up to me.

25

KADENCE

I pulled up and parked in the driveway.

"What is Auntie Jazzy doing here?" Kai asked. I turned and saw her car parked on the street. I hadn't noticed it before.

"I don't know. Let's go find out." The further along I got, the more I had to use the bathroom. I didn't remember peeing half as much when I was pregnant with Kai. I ran into the house and straight to the bathroom. I heard Kai come in and turn the TV on. Bryson wasn't in the living room, so I figured he was upstairs in his man cave. I went back outside to get the bags that I knew Kai had abandoned in the car. I looked over at Jazelle's car. She wasn't inside. I walked back into the house and put the groceries away.

"Kai, are you sure that's Auntie Jazzy's car?" Kai looked out the window and nodded her head.

"Yeah, I'm sure. She was driving it at granny's house yesterday. I remember because I said I wanted one of those when I get old enough to drive." I nodded my head.

"Okay, I'll be right back. I'm going to go change clothes." Kai was already focused on her tablet and paying me no mind. I walked up the stairs and paused outside of my bedroom door. I had a sharp pain in my stomach. After waiting a few seconds, I shook it off and opened the door. Bryson was lying there with his eyes closed. There was a huge lump under the covers.

"What the fuck?" I whispered, but it was loud enough for Jazelle to pop up from underneath the covers.

"Oh shit!" Bryson never moved. He kept his eyes closed. "Kadence let me explain."

"You ain't gone ever learn are you bitch?" I turned and walked away. "Kai, come on. Let's go to granny's house." I slammed the door behind me and walked down the steps.

"I thought we were gonna make lunch."

"We are, but I need to talk to mama about something. I forgot to stop there on the way home." I grabbed her hand and practically dragged her out of the house. I tried to fight the urge to cry, but my hormones got the best of me.

"Mommy? Are you okay?" Kai stopped walking and pulled her hand away from me.

"Yeah, I'm fine." She looked back at the house.

"People who are fine, don't cry. You can tell me. I'm a big girl." I smiled at my baby. I admired her for her strength. With everything that she was going through, she was still trying to be there for me. That alone let me know that I was doing something right.

"I'm okay baby." I walked towards the car, and she followed behind me.

I had tried to give Jazelle the benefit of the doubt. I was thinking that maybe she had just lost her way with all the changes that she had been going through, but now I was certain that she had lost her motherfuckin' mind. If she was paranoid about me changing the plan and leaving her out of it, she had definitely made the wrong move for that. I made it to my mother's house in record time. Kenedee was sitting on the porch smoking when I pulled up. She was grinning from ear to ear, but her smile faded when I got out of the car.

"I need you to watch Kai." I walked Kai to the porch and turned to go back to the car. Kai and Kenedee watched from the porch.

"Wait Kay; I wanna talk to you about something."

"I'll be right back." I just back in the car and sped back to my house.

I don't know what the hell Jazelle was doing in my house or what the fuck Bryson was thinking fuckin' around with her in my mother-fuckin' bed! My blood was boiling. I could feel the slight flutters from the baby moving around. My heart felt like it would beat out of my chest. I pulled into the driveway surprised to see that both of them were still there. Throwing caution out the window, I grabbed my .9mm and silencer from the drawer in the foyer. I tightened the silencer as I made my way up the stairs. I could hear them arguing from the other side of the door.

"Kadence is going to fuckin' kill you! You have to leave." Bryson laughed.

"Kadence ain't gonna kill me."

"She is she told me! That's why I'm here, to help." I pushed the door open and watched as they ran around the room, getting dressed. Bryson made eye contact with me at the door but said nothing. I pushed the door open a little more the end of my gun.

"Bryson, you have to come with me."

"Was this just a sick plan to try to get me back?" Bryson stared at Jazelle. His back was to the door, blocking Jazelle from seeing me. I inched into the room a little more and waited.

"Kadence doesn't fuckin' deserve you! She's lost her fuckin' mind since Loyal died, and if you stay with her, you're gonna end up just like his ass."

"Bryson is not going any fuckin' where with you." I stepped inside the room completely. My .9 pointed at Jazelle. "Sit down!" I kept the gun pointed at her. Both, Jazelle and Bryson had their hands raised and moved slowly to the bed.

"Kadence, baby, what are you doing?"

"Don't baby me, motherfucka! I knew it! I knew you were still fuckin' around with her!" I screamed. My head was pounding, and it was obvious that my emotions were getting the best of me, but I didn't care.

"Kadence, it ain't what you think."

"I think that me and my child walked in on you two bitches." I waved the gun between them. "Fucking in MY motherfuckin' bed! I cocked my gun and focused on Bryson. "Tell me I'm wrong, babe." I could see the nervousness in his eyes. Déjà vu of the night Loyal died set in.

"You're wrong, Kay!" Jazelle now fully dressed yelled from the other side of the room.

"Bitch, who asked you? And didn't I tell you to sit the fuck down?" Jazelle took a seat on the bed, her hands still raised in the air. I sat down next to her and pointed the gun at Bryson.

"Tell me this, why can't motherfuckas ever stick to the goddamn plan? Now, I feel like you two had a plan that didn't include me. Jazzy, you know how much I hate being left out. " I looked over at Jazelle, and she was crying. The nerve of that bitch!

"Kay, just let me explain." Bryson began taking a step closer towards me.

"Okay, make it make sense." I stood and motioned for him to take my seat next to Jazelle. "Go ahead. I'm listening, baby." I smiled at Bryson. His eyes were as wide a doorknob, and he was sweating bullets.

"I couldn't get her off." Bryson shrugged his shoulders, and I couldn't help but laugh. I scratched my head because I knew that he had to be fuckin' kidding me! That could not have been his final fuckin' answer.

"Come on, Bryson! I know you're supposed to be a good dude and all, but I know you can lie better than that."

Jazelle was fidgeting and scratching herself all over. "Stop moving! I'll blow your shit wide the fuck open!" Both of them looked at me, shocked. I guess they didn't get the memo that pushover Kadence was gone. "Give me your phone." Jazelle handed me her phone, her hands trembling. I sent a text to my phone.

Jazelle: Kay, I'm so sorry for everything. I should have never messed around with Loyal. Do me a favor, and tell mama I'm sorry. I fixed it the best way I knew how.

"Kadence, calm down; think about the baby."

"Oh, I'm thinking about my baby, are you? Did you think about our baby when you were fuckin' this bitch in my motherfuckin' bed? You don't even live here!" I screamed at Bryson. I was starting to feel lightheaded, so I toned it down a little.

"You got it all wrong, Kadence," Jazelle started.

"You know what, I'm over it." I sat down on the left side of Jazelle and put the gun to her head. "I need you to understand that you are not about to die because you betrayed me. I'm killing you because of how you tried to play my mother bitch. We trusted you, Jazzy." I couldn't stop the tears that had begun to fall from my eyes.

"Kadence, I'm sorry, sis." I pulled the trigger, and Jazelle's brains painted the wall. I looked up at Bryson. His mouth was hanging wide open.

"Did you really have to fuck her in my bed, B?" He shrugged his shoulders and wiped the sweat from his face.

"You said, do whatever I had to do." We laughed.

Bryson handed me a clean shirt. I changed and put the gun in Jazelle's hand. I stared at her lifeless body and surprisingly, I didn't feel one ounce of remorse.

"You ready?" Bryson asked, handing me a towel to clean my face.

"Yeah." I took a deep breath and dialed 911.

"Hello? I need an ambulance!" I said in a panic. I forced tears from my eyes. "I got this strange text from my sister, and then I came home to find her not breathing in my bed! Oh my god! Somebody come help my sister!" I played the role well. Bryson stared at me in disbelief as tears slid down my face. I gave the dispatcher my address and waited.

"What happened to your sister?"

"She shot herself! Oh, there's blood everywhere!" I cried and threw up on the floor.

"Ma'am? I need you to leave the room. Is there anyone else there with you?"

"Yes, there's someone here."

"Okay, I need you and whoever is there with you to go wait outside. Emergency personnel are on the way." I smiled and checked myself in the mirror. After I was certain there was nothing that could pinpoint me as Jazelle's killer, I walked out on the porch and ended the call. I could hear sirens, so it was only a matter of time before they made it. Bryson put his hands on both of my shoulders.

"You know you had me a little worried in there." I leaned my head back into his chest.

"I hope you took notes."

"Notes? Baby, I'm King B, ever heard of me?" I shook my head.

"But, I know for a fact, Krazy Kay is not to be fucked with." Bryson laughed and kissed the top of my head.

"We make a hell of a team, don't we baby?"

"Yes, we definitely do." Several squad cars pulled up and swarmed my house. I cried dramatically on Bryson's shoulder, while they did their jobs. The same detective that had been working Loyal's case walked over to us.

"I'm so sorry for your loss."

"Thank you."

"Mrs. Jackson, I wanted to personally tell you that with the death of our prime suspect, your husband's case has been closed. I hope you find some sort of closure in all of this." He nodded his head at Bryson before walking away.

"Maybe we should go break the news to mama?" I said loudly. A female officer rushed to my side.

"Do you need a ride?" She smiled down at the small bulge under my shirt.

"No, thank you. My boyfriend is here. I have to check on my daughter. Jazzy was her favorite aunt." I wiped the tears from my face, as Bryson helped me into the car.

"You should have been a fuckin' actress.'"

"Why, thank you. Thank you very much." I slid my sunglasses on as Bryson maneuvered through the chaos. Mama would be sad, but I knew getting rid of Jazelle would turn out to be best for everybody.

∾

WHEN BRYSON and I pulled up, Kenedee was still on the porch, but this time she wasn't alone.

"Hey y'all! I've been waiting for y'all to get back. Kenedee was more excited than I had ever seen her. "Mama! Kai! Come here!" she screamed loudly in my ear.

"Kenedee, what the hell?" Mama walked into the front room with Kai right behind her.

"What's all the commotion for?" Zane and Kenedee smiled like teenagers who were given the car for the first time without a parent.

"We're married!" Kenedee held up her hand and showed up the humongous ring on her finger.

"Shut the hell up! I just saw you earlier, and you weren't married!" I examined the ring that looked like it could break her tiny finger any second.

"I wasn't then, but I am now. And I want you to meet my husband, Detective Zane Michaels." A lump formed in my throat. What the hell was she doing running around with a fuckin' detective, let alone married to one?

"Congrats, Auntie Ken!" Kai was the first to speak. She ran up and gave Kenedee and hug. "And, it's nice to meet you, Uncle Zane." Zane kneeled to Kai's level and smiled.

"I've never had a niece before, so maybe you can show me how to be a great uncle."

"Money always works," Kai said with a mischievous grin on her face.

"Um, Kenedee can I talk to you in the other room please?" Kenedee was reluctant to let Zane go, so I literally dragged her.

"A fuckin' cop, Ken? Really?"

"He knew too much, Kay! What the fuck else was I supposed to do?"

"I don't know, maybe not fuckin' tell him everything! How could you do that, Ken?"

"I'm protecting us."

"Protecting us? Or yourself? Cuz this shit doesn't make sense to

me." I tried to keep my voice low, but today had been too fuckin;
stressful.

"He cannot testify against us if he's my husband." I sat down on
the bed and stared at her.

"Ken, baby there's more to it than that."

"It was fine when you married Loyal right out of high school. A
broke ass wannabe singer. But, I marry a detective, and everybody has
a fuckin' problem."

"I'm not saying that. I'm just saying you're believing everything he
says like police ain't the biggest criminals in the fuckin' world."

"He's not even checkin' for you. He wants Jazelle."

"Jazelle is dead."

"She's what?" Mama stood in the doorway with her hand over
her heart.

"Jazelle commuted suicide a few hours ago," I repeated while
staring at Kenedee. "That's why I'm here. To tell you I found
her body."

"Found her body?" Kenedee folded her arms across her chest. I
nodded my head and walked over to my Mama.

"Where was she?" I cleared my throat.

"She shot herself with my gun, in my bed." It rolled off my tongue
so easily. "The police are there now."

"And they let you leave?" Kenedee said with a little too much
sarcasm in her voice.

"You got a problem, Kenedee? Say that shit!" I walked towards
her.

"Yeah, I think you're full of shit!"

26

ZANE

There was an uncomfortable silence in the room. I extended my hand to the only other man I had seen around Kenedee and her family.

"So, I'm Zane." He looked around the room as if I could have been talking to anyone else.

"Whassup man, I'm Bryson." We shook hands.

"So are you and Kadence married?" I asked, trying to make conversation. Bryson stared at me. Something about him was familiar to me, but I couldn't quite put my finger on it.

"Naw. We're engaged though. No offense, but I have to ask what made you marry Kenedee?" He leaned forward never taking his eyes off me.

"I love her, and I don't ever want to be without her again." I shrugged my shoulders.

My intentions with Kenedee were good. For some reason, I wanted to keep her out of trouble. What better protection could there have been than me? Bryson looked like he was sizing me up. He nodded his head, never taking his eyes off me.

"How long you been a cop?" I noticed the way he frowned his face when he said cop.

"A little over six years. I did the carpet cleaning shit before that." I told him loosening up my tie. "You got something against cops?" I stared back at him. Bryson raised his hands in the air.

"At the end of the day, you just a man doing his job. Why would I have a problem with that?" I tried my best to figure out what was so familiar about him.

"I think you're full of shit!" Kenedee screamed from the next room. I glanced in that direction and then back at Bryson.

"You think we should go in there?" I tilted my head towards the hall. Bryson shook his head.

"Ken is a passionate person. She's always yelling about something."

There was a loud crash followed by Kadence calling for help. Bryson and I ran towards the noise. Kenedee and Kadence were hunched over Ms. Lena who was laid out on the floor. I rushed to her side and checked her pulse. Her pulse was weak, and she was unresponsive. I pulled out my phone and called for an ambulance.

"Is she okay?" Kenedee asked. Her eyes were wide, and she was on the verge of tears. "I can't lose my mama, Zane."

"She's gonna be fine. Why don't you and Kadence go out and wait for the EMTs." I looked up at Bryson.

"Yeah, come on ladies. The detective got this." He ushered them out of the room. A few seconds later, Bryson came back. "Is she okay?" It was clear to me that he was worried.

"I think she just got a little overwhelmed. Help me get her to the bed." Bryson walked over and together, we lifted her up and into the bed. I looked out the window and saw the ambulance pulling up. A few seconds later, Kenedee returned with my other sister, Syia.

"Whassup bro? It's nice to finally hear from you." I hugged her and pointed to Ms. Lena who still had not woke up.

"I'm sorry. I was on a case. How you been?" Kenedee stared at Syia and me. "I'm so sorry. This is my older sister, Syia. Syia this is my wife, Kenedee, her sister Kadence, and her fiancé, Bryson." Syia waved and walked over to access Ms. Lena.

"How many sisters do you have?" Kenedee asked as I wrapped my arm around her and escorted her out of the room. The sun was setting, and it was my favorite time of day. I tried to walk her out on the porch, but Kadence didn't let us make it that far.

"Ain't that something you should know before you get married?" She rolled her eyes and sat down on the couch.

"Please let's not talk about what motherfuckas should have been aware of before they said I do." Kenedee turned around and pulled away from me. "Maybe you wouldn't be so damn paranoid now." I stepped in front of Kenedee.

"Kadence, I think you may have misunderstood this, uh arrangement that Kenedee and I have." Kenedee folded her arms and stared at Kadence.

"Okay, so maybe you can explain it to me." Kadence stared at me. Those gray eyes held a dangerous look.

"I'm not here for you. I don't care about anything that you, or you..." I turned and looked at Bryson. "Have done. I'm here because I love Kenedee, and just like anybody in love when she called I came running. I'm just as guilty as any of you in this room. The way I see it, we can help each other. You don't speak on anything concerning me, and I won't speak on anything concerning anyone in this family. I got word that Jazelle Green was found dead and that was the person I initially came for. So, everything is good. I may be a cop, but I'm a useful one to have on your team." Kadence smiled, but Bryson looked skeptical.

"How are we supposed to know that you ain't still undercover? That all this ain't a setup?"

"If I was going to tell, I would have told when I replaced the floors for y'all. Did you really think the differences in the blood didn't show? Why do you think I replaced the whole floor? I mean it was a great idea, but had I not been looking out for you in the beginning, you would have been in jail." Kadence nodded her head and looked up at Bryson.

"Are you married?" Kadence asked.

"To Kenedee, yes." Kenedee laughed, and Kadence rolled her eyes.

"My sister had always moved a little fast in relationships. Last I knew, she never wanted to get married. Two days later here you come with a diamond ring and everything changes. It just don't seem legit," Kenedee spoke up.

"We went to the justice of the peace a few hours ago. It's legit, and I really don't feel like I have to explain any of this to you. What happened to being happy for me?" Kadence stood up and walked over to Kenedee.

"Okay, baby girl. If you're happy, then I'm happy for you."

"And one more thing." Kenedee pulled Kadence into a hug.

"What's that, sis?"

"Never call me baby girl again." They both burst into laughter. Syia walked out with a smile on her face.

"Your mom is fine. She missed her medication this morning and got a little overwhelmed. She said she just needs to rest before the big move."

"Move?" I turned and looked at Kenedee. "Where is she going?"

"Mama bought a house in Texas. We were planning to move next week." I smiled.

"Texas seems like a good idea." Kenedee jumped into my arms and kissed me.

"See Kadence; I love this man." Both of our sisters looked at each other. Both of their eyes filled with skepticism.

"Okay. I'm going to go lay down." Kadence rubbed her belly and walked up the hall with Bryson right behind her. Syia and Kenedee were deep in conversation about something. I smiled and sat down to check my phone.

Captain: Congrats on the wedding.

Me: Thank you, sir.

Captain: Everything still on schedule?

Me: Yes, no worries. We're moving to Texas.

Captain: I'll put in the paperwork.

For the past four years, my captain and I had been trafficking drugs. Moving to Texas would only help our operation grow. I worked the undercover cases and then took out the competition, which is why having a wife like Kenedee by my side was the best idea. I knew she could hold her own and have my back. Kadence had groomed her perfectly, and now I was ready to make her untouchable. Bryson walked back in the living room and smiled.

"Are you a drinking man, Zane?"

"Yeah, what you got?" I followed him into the kitchen. He grabbed a bottle of Henny from the freezer and poured both of us a double shot.

"You look really familiar to me, Bryson." I downed my shot and poured another.

"I guess I just have one of those faces."

"Yeah. Maybe. What do you do for a living?"

"A little bit of everything," Bryson said nonchalantly.

"Well, I may have a job for you in Texas, if you don't mind getting your hands dirty." Bryson shrugged his shoulders while pouring himself another shot.

"A little hard work never hurt nobody." I smiled. My brother-in-law and I were going to get along just fine. When the time was right, I would lay everything on the table, but for now, We would start small.

"I was hoping you would say that." Kenedee and Syia came in and poured shots as well.

"Here's to new beginnings," I said. Everyone touched their glasses together.

"Well, I have to get back to work, but as soon as you're settled call me, and I will come visit," Syia said as she hugged Kenedee.

"I sure will. He will get better with keeping in touch." I hugged my sister goodbye as I walked her to the door.

"Are you sure this the right girl for this? She seems kind of blonde." Syia said shrugging her shoulders.

"Trust me; she's perfect. It's all an act." I watched Syia walk back to her ambulance, then joined Kenedee and Bryson in the kitchen. They were deep in conversation until I walked in.

"Don't stop on my account."

"Bryson was just telling about them finding Jazelle. She committed suicide." I sat down and watched Bryson.

"Damn, nobody knows why?" His body language screamed that Jazelle had not killed herself.

"Something about fixing things the best she knew how." I nodded my head.

"Usually when people cause so much trouble in their family's lives, they think death is the only way to right their wrongs." Kenedee rolled her eyes.

"Lord, forgive me, but I'm glad the bitch is gone." Bryson excused himself. Kenedee and I sat at the table, getting more acquainted than we had done over the past few weeks.

"So, what do you think of my family?" Kenedee asked, taking a sip from her glass that she had upgraded to.

"I think we are going to get along just fine." I kissed her forehead and smiled. "Everything will be just fine.

27

KADENCE

ix Months Later

S I woke up to the sun blazing through the skylight over my bed. I rolled over and kissed Bryson.

"Morning, babe."

"Good morning, gorgeous."

I sat up and walked over to the bassinet in the corner of the room. Our three-week-old son, Kannon slept peacefully. I changed his diaper and went to the bathroom. When I came back, Bryson was sitting in his "daddy chair" feeding Kannon.

"You guys are so cute!" I couldn't stop the feelings growing inside of me. The birth of my first son had me beyond emotional, but the bond that he and Bryson shared was nothing but amazing. Whenever he cried, Bryson was there. Whenever he wanted to be held, daddy to the rescue. Most times, I found myself feeling useless because Kannon literally wanted for nothing.

"What you got planned today?" Zane asked, laying Kannon over his shoulder to burp him.

"Zane's transfer finally went through, so Kenedee is arriving today." I couldn't stop smiling. I was really in a happy place. I had never gone without seeing my sister for more than two weeks at a time, and I missed her in the worst way.

"So we might as well count mommy out for the next few hours," Bryson joked and placed Kannon back in his bassinet. He walked over to me and pulled me close. Bryson kissed me passionately, lifting me off my feet in the process.

"Those six weeks got to be up by now, right?" I laughed and pushed him away.

"You know it's not. You're just going to have to control your hormones."

I went to take a shower. When I came back, both Kannon and Bryson were gone. I pulled a hot pink maxi dress from the closet and slipped it over my head. I went downstairs to find them on the couch watching football, something that Bryson had been addicted to since moving to Texas. I walked into the kitchen to make breakfast. A few seconds later, mama and Kai stumbled into the kitchen.

"Good morning, mama." Kai ran over and kissed my cheek the same way that she did every morning. Mama started a pot of coffee.

"Hey baby, Are you ready for school?"

Kai had decided that she was too old to be dropped off by me. She begged to carpool with some of the other kids from the neighborhood. With a lot of help from Bryson, I finally agreed. Kai poured a glass of milk and sat down at the table.

"I'm a big girl, mom. You don't have to keep tabs on me." At almost 11 years old, my child thought she had life all figured out. I turned to mama and sat her egg whites in front of her.

"Mama, are you going with me to pick Kenedee up from the airport?" Mama shook her head.

"You know I don't fool with them people."

When we first moved here, the airport had lost Mama's luggage and half a year later. She still had not received everything that was missing, and she held the workers at the airport responsible. Bryson walked in and took his seat at the head of the table.

"Good morning, ladies," he said as Kannon was snatched from his arms. Mama and Kai gushed over how cute he was while Bryson stared at me.

The doorbell rang, and of course, no one moved to answer it. I turned the stove down and went to answer the door. I opened it, and Kenedee stood there with a huge smile on her face. Huge sunglasses covered her eyes. Kenedee was wearing a dress almost identical to mine.

"Surprise!" she yelled and threw her hands in the air. I pulled her into a hug and screamed.

"Oh my God! I wasn't supposed to pick you up for another couple of hours! What are you doing here? Look at you." Kenedee was certainly thicker than the last time I saw her. Marriage had definitely been treating her well.

"I wanted to surprise you." She grabbed my hand and pulled me out on the porch. "Surprise again! We're neighbors!" She pointed at the house directly across the street from mine. There were moving trucks parked along the street and men moving boxes inside the house.

"Yay!" We screamed and jumped up and down together. "Come inside! You have to meet Kannon." Kenedee ran past me towards the kitchen.

"Hey family!" she said loudly.

Kai was the first to run and hug her. Kenedee hugged her tightly and whispered in her ear. Kai nodded her head as she ran upstairs to grab her book bag and then out of the house. Kenedee pushed her glasses on her head and walked over to Bryson.

"Hey, B. How you been?" she asked, giving him a half hug while taking Kannon from his arms.

"I've been chillin'. How about you, Ken?"

"I'm great!" she said, making funny faces at Kannon.

"And mama?" She turned and kissed her on the cheek. Mama stood and hugged Kenedee tight.

"I've missed you so much, Kenedee."

"I missed you too, mama. How you been feeling?" Mama gave Kenedee a rundown of everything she had missed in the past few months. I walked back on the porch and saw the mailman coming up the sidewalk.

"Morning, Ms. Jones."

"Morning, honey." I smiled as the young girl handed me my mail.

I flipped through the bills until my eyes landed on an envelope that had unmistakable handwriting. The envelope was addressed to me from Jazelle. The hairs on the back of my neck stood on end. I opened it, and a card fell out. It was a card that said, "Wish you were here" in dark red letters. I opened the card, and a check for $50,000 made out to me fell out.

Kadence, You deserve everything that is coming to you. Be careful, sis. Love J.

I walked off the porch and looked up and down the block. A part of me expected Jazelle to hop out of the bushes on my ass. I shook my head and walked back into the house. I sat on the bed and stared at the envelope. It was postmarked for two days ago. Kenedee knocked on the door before coming inside.

"Is everything okay, Kay?" I showed her the card. Kendee's eye got wide. She pulled a similar card from her purse.

"Oh my god! This came to the house a few days ago. I didn't think nothing of it because Zane assured me that she was dead and gone. It's weird though, right?" I nodded my head.

"Is that all she sent you?" Kenedee nodded her head. The huge smile she wore before was now replaced with worry.

"Why? What else did she send you?"

"A check for $50, 000." Kenedee pulled out her phone and called Zane.

"Babe, you did see Jazelle's body right?" She put him on speaker and stared at me.

"Yes. I was there when she was cremated. Why what's wrong?"

"Kadence got a letter from her too and a check."

"Hey Kadence, you have nothing to worry about. I'll be there in a few days, and we will get to the bottom of this. "

"Thanks, bro."

Once I got past the initial shock of Kenedee being married, Zane and I became friends, and he had proved time and time again that it was good to have someone on the other side of the law on your team. I decided not to show the letter to Bryson for fear that I would never be able to leave the house again. I got up and stared out the window, trying to figure out what Jazelle had up her sleeve. Knowing that Zane had personally seen her cremated made me feel a little better, but not enough that I didn't need to be prepared. I called Devon, and she answered on the first ring.

"What's good, Kay?"

"You wanna make a trip?"

"Whatever you need." I smiled and rambled off a list of items I needed. "Damn sis, are you going to war or something?"

"You never know." I lit a blunt and passed it to Kenedee. "But, if I am bitch I will be ready for whatever." I hung up and smiled. "Punk ass Kadence is gone."

THE END

THANKS

I can't believe my fifth book is complete! Thank y'all so much for rocking with me! Be sure to screenshot proof of purchase and review and send it to Jasmine Akins on Facebook for you chance to win a free Amazon Gift Card!

MORE BOOKS BY JAZ' AKINS:

LOVE CAN BE A DANGEROUS GAME

Forbidden: I Was Never Supposed To Love You
Taking His Heart and His Throne
Taking His Heart and His Throne 2 (10/28/17)
Thank you for your support!

CPSIA information can be obtained
at www.ICGtesting.com
Printed in the USA
LVOW13s1918071117
555373LV00014B/1383/P